KITTY MORGAN

FAILURE IN TIME

TINY TREE

Failure in Time
Published in 2025 by
Tiny Tree Books
West Wing Studios
Unit 166, The Mall
Luton, LU1 2TL
tinytreebooks.com

For mum and dad, without whom
I could never have written this book

ACKNOWLEDGEMENTS

To my mum and dad, for the lockdown zooms and a lifetime of love. Without you, this book would not exist, and nor would I.

To the wider sibling clique inc. Nad, I am forever grateful for a lifetime of creative inspiration, laughter, and picking up the pieces.

Thanks as always to the best in-laws in the world, Annie, Andy, Penny, and the eternal spirit of Clive.

To my early readers of this novel: Edward, Bonner, Nad and Ben L: thank you, you legends.

To the team at Tiny Tree and Andrews UK, especially my editor James, for believing in Failure and giving her life.

To my agent Rachel Daniels for your unwavering support.

To Diane Samuels, in whose extraordinary writing group I first discovered Failure.

To my extended chosen family of Claire and James, Neil, Catherine, Amy, Rosie, Ads, Helena, Katie, Em, the Trumps, Corbyns and Roberts - I couldn't be luckier to have you, it was in missing you so throughout lockdown that this world was born.

And to Ben, Alfie and Casper, for filling my life with more love than I thought existed in this time, all the times before, and all the times beyond x

PART ONE
THE JOURNEY

CHAPTER ONE

Failure stood in the mouth of the dark alleyway and stared at her target, all determination and grit, in her jeans shorts, wellies and bright yellow raincoat. Pulling her black sou'wester hat from her head, she held it in a small, determined fist. Strands of filthy, ash-coloured hair prickled as they clung to the sheen of sweat on her forehand and a devilish grin crept upon her green-stained lips. In just a few breaths' time she would complete her first ever Task for him. She would prove herself at last. She would become a thief.

It was almost midday, but the sky above was dark as night. Here in London Under glimpses of the sun were rare, blocked out as they were by the dense black smog clouds which filled the skies. And although the streetlamps were glowing honey-yellow, burning their whale oil fuel, Failure's world was as gloomy as ever. A land of shadows.

All the better to go unseen, Failure whispered silently to her guts, grinning.

Yeah, but it's muggy out here today and you know what that means, her guts grumbled back. *You should've worn more than a rain mac and shorts.*

It'll be fine, don't panic me. Failure snapped. *We're here now. It's good and dark. Doesn't look like there's any Guzzers out on the beat round here. So, it's all lined up. I just need to get the Task done and get the heck back to Fitzrovia.*

But a storm's coming, her guts insisted. *And if you're caught out in it, you'll get burned or worse. You're too used to the easy shelter back home. It's made you careless.*

Yeah, well if I have to find a place to hold out then I've got my Zeeva with me. The one Pa gave me on my fifteenth Winter Solstice.

Best crossbow on the black market. That'll help persuade some do-gooder to let me in.

Of course, but it'd be more use in your hands than strapped to your back, her guts grumbled again.

Well, we aren't in Fitzrovia now, Failure sighed. *They wear their weapons on their backs or their belts here in Greenwich, and I have to look like one of them. Just another London Under girl out enjoying the festival of Samhain, the day of the dead.*

The street beyond was filled with them; the normal folks out to enjoy the festival, or heading home from the dawn shifts on the river; ballast heavers, who loaded the ships at the Greenwich docks, all of them thick with muscle, weather worn, hunched and stained with old sweat; little mud larks who salvaged scrap from the riverbanks at low tide; street kids, dancing and howling before their begging bowls in masks made from scrap; fishermen, priestesses, rope-makers, merchants and far too many dogs.

A cockle-picker jangled past lugging her heavy, rattling baskets on blackened feet and missing toes; they made good money, the cockle-pickers did, but the Water Blight always took its toll in the end. It had started at the time of the Great Quake. Pa had told her all about it, for she had only been a baby when it happened.

The Great Quake had shattered an area of the Artic ice cap known as Hadrovane, throwing it into the sea. There were months of flash floods, fires and earthquakes, panic and death and devastation. If the Kala had not taken control of Britain at that time, Pa explained, then the Goddess only knew what would have become of them.

In the years that followed, the rain began to sting, sometimes burn. The skin on the workers' legs blackened and their toes were taken off by the salt-bite. The river water grew sticky and heavy. Lights began appearing under the waves. There was more down there these days than treasure and fish. Mrs Flaherty from the third floor had seen something slinking its way through Gt Norman Street with the ease of a big cat or an alligator, some kind of doll clapped in its jaws. And poor dead Harry Fulcher had been hunted by a pack of hungry dogs, who only backed off when he waded out into the flood. Failure hadn't been able to swim for years, and she missed it more than almost anything.

Enough regretting, her guts cut in. *Get on with it before the storm comes.*

Mumma Dory's Chowder Cafe. It stood on the opposite side of the street from Failure's alleyway. A group of fishermen swaggered toward the steamed-up windows and with the jangling of a bell, they flung the door open and jostled inside. A cloud of white steam consumed them and a mouthwatering scent of freshly baked bread and smoked haddock seeped across the street to Failure.

Perhaps a little drop of lichen-tox might settle the nerves? her guts suggested.

Stop banging on like I'm nervous, Failure replied. But all the same, she used her nails to rip a chunk of damp lichen from the wall at her side and sucked the fungus like a sponge. The familiar tingle in the knees came, as the poisonous lichen-tox sizzled through her skin. Soothing. Deadly, if you drank too deeply.

See, that's better, her guts chimed. Failure spat out the toxic juice and stepped out into the dark of the street.

The shops to either side of the Chowder Cafe were long since abandoned. One had been smothered with an enormous Time Corp billboard, which was peeling and sagging in the muggy air.

"Futility Watanabe!" Read the words in once-glorious golden ink. "The Kala salutes you! Go bravely in the past!" The girl smiled down with impossibly white teeth and glossy black hair. She was dressed in the Time Programme Uniform: grey t-shirt, black shorts and black trainers. The sun-kissed skin of her arms, legs and neck was painted in dozens of Triumph tattoos, each image representing one of Futility's many achievements at the Time Programme; a grandfather clock, maps, mathematical sequences, a girl running, a campfire, images of the Goddess. Futility had one hand on her hip, the other raised before her, forefinger pointing to the sky, sending her luck to the Kala.

No goddam smog grits crusting your eyes and nose, Futility Watanabe, Failure thought wryly, rubbing the corners of her own brown eyes clear of black grits and wincing as the sting of the lichen tox residue on her finger momentarily blinded her. *No ricket-laced brittle bones and bowed legs for you, either. You didn't come from round here. Anyway, wish me luck. And good luck back at you, whenever you are.*

It had been more than a year since the city had been air-dropped with thousands of flyers announcing Futility Watanabe's Travelling. But there had been no word of her since, and still the waters rose. Whenever she had gone back to, and whatever she had done back there, it was yet to save them.

With a gush of steam, an elderly woman hobbled out of the chowder cafe, dressed head to toe in a long brown mackintosh and an oversized sou'wester. The older ones couldn't take any risks with the burning rain. Fizzing with lichen-tox courage, Failure called, "Hey, m'love, is Jada's eldest lad in there today? What's his name? Shame, isn't it?"

Peering from under the wide brim of her hat, the woman fixed Failure with eyes thickly crusted with smog grit. "I hope you ain't looking for a boyfriend on the day of the dead, kiddy? That's bad luck."

"Maybe I am or maybe I'm not."

"You'll bring the shadow on y'self," the old woman warned. "An' they're all big trouble, Jada's lads are, knows you."

"Maybe I like a bit of trouble," Failure grinned.

"And you look like it's that way too," the woman growled with a shadowy smile. "And one thing's sure and done for girls like you; you'll meet with trouble, so you will. Kala protect you."

"She always does," Failure laughed, raising a forefinger to the sky. "So, Jada's eldest in there or not? Or any of them in there, m'love?"

"Not as I saw it, kiddy," the woman replied. "Better you go home." She limped away, her laboured gait marking her as a some-time cockle-picker. Failure gritted her teeth. Then approached.

The cafe was stiflingly hot and raucous with chatter and the smell of smoked fish. The bell jangled as Failure entered, but no one gave the fair-haired girl with pale skin and black freckles a second glance. Jada was stirring a vat of bubbling chowder in a huge metal pan. Six feet two, with pendulous breasts and fleshy arms, her long black braids woven with silver thread and oyster shells, Jada sang, like the chief of a fairytale Mermaid clan, as she stirred and wiped sweat from her brow.

"Mug of tea with bean milk, m'lovely," Failure smiled.

"Four hundred Quid, kiddy," Jada smiled back, displaying gaps in her gums, where several gold teeth had been, before the Claiming. In the back room beyond, an elderly man sat in the back doorway in a rocking chair. He was chewing on laced squid skin and humming tunelessly. Rows and rows of shelves surrounded him, lined with a library of dead river life; glass jars of jellied whelks and eels, salted crabs, mussels in shells, fish eyeballs and bones for stock. In the centre of this macabre library stood a large metal island, where a solitary oil lamp flickered beside a knife block and a questionable hunk of greying seal blubber. And a small black box. Silver handle. Silver lock. Just as Pa had described it.

All I have to do is snatch that box and sprint out of the back door, Failure told her guts. *Easy.*

What if there's someone out there on the back street though? her guts worried. *Or if it's a dead end? You should've checked the goddam back street first. And there's an old bloke right in the way.*

He won't be any trouble.

As though he had heard her, the old man's eyes turned towards Failure, milk-white with cataracts. "You smells of lime soapy wash, girl," he called to her in a thick London Under accent. "Where you get such strong soapy wash, except the black market, eh?"

"I can get you three bars for five hundred thousand quid?" Failure called back brazenly. "Treat yourself today, it's the festival of the dead, isn't it?"

"I remembers my dead every day," he muttered and went back to sucking his squid skin.

"Anything else for you?" Jada asked, thumping a chipped mug onto the counter.

"Yeah, you uh… you got any shifts going?" Failure asked, trying to sound casual despite the fizz of lichen tox in her fingertips and the pounding heart in her chest.

Jada peered up at Failure from under thick black lashes. "You asking me for work, kiddy?" She asked in a velvety voice.

"Yes m'love. Anything to stay off the mud flats this winter," Failure replied, feeling like an actress on stage in the music hall and thoroughly enjoying her own show. "I don't want the salt-bite to rot my toes off. I'm only sixteen, I've got a lot of dancing to do, can't be hobbling about without my toes. I'm a good worker though m'love. Won't mess you about. Sell a load of chowder and tea and all that. Charm up the clients better than your own Futility Watanabe, your own Penitence McCleod. You give me a trial today, I'll show you my salt-grit, no problem."

"And why," Jada smiled a dangerous smile, "is Pa Townhouse's little snip asking me for work so far south of Fitzrovia? And on a festival day? Didn't think I knew who you were? Girl with ashy white hair, green-tinged lips and a three-bolt Zeeva crossbow strapped to her back."

She's on to you.

Failure's mind felt sharp, glassy, white-hot. She licked her lips self-consciously; she tasted the smoky kiss of chowder; the bitterness of smog, the sharp salt of the estuary and the distant tang of seaweed, always under it all. It was the seaweed that had saved her from the Water Blight and marked her lips, perhaps forever, with its stain and a shadow of its taste. It had betrayed her more than once in the nine years since. Yes, she had survived, which was a rare thing. But the Troubles she had experienced since had been the cost. Pa had helped her to hide them. If the folks had ever known that Failure had been in any way *Changed*, then they would have come for her; they would have been right to. So, Pa, despite what he was to so many others, had been her saviour.

I'd rather die trying than fail Pa. Failure told her guts.

You probably will, they sighed.

Failure grabbed the scalding mug of tea and flung the contents at Jada, who screamed in fury and ducked away. She slipped, crashing to the ground like a fallen giantess. Failure leapt past her and sprinted into to the back room, even as Jada screamed, "Lads! Shame! All of you here, now!"

Failure snatched the black box from the metal island, shocked to find it extraordinarily heavy for its size. Clinging it to her chest, she ran for the open back door. But the old man lurched forwards and whipped his cane at Failure so fast that the air whistled, slicing the bare skin above her knee like a blade. Overbalancing from his own attack, the old man sprawled on the floor, snatching for Failure's ankles like a piranha. Failure stamped at him with her heavy brown boots and made good contact with his shoulder blade, which gave with a splintering crack. He cried out, curling up like a child as, clutching the black box to her chest, Failure fled into the dark of the back street.

CHAPTER TWO

You need to get into the festival crowds! Failure's guts screamed, as she pounded down the paving slabs. Urgent voices were yelling behind her; Jada's lads had begun their pursuit. Failure emerged beside the Time Corp billboard.

Lucky I'm fast as a cat with a burning tail, hey, Futility Watanabe? Failure laughed, racing through the crowds.

That Task was a shambles, her guts admonished furiously. *You barely had a plan. We were lucky to get out alive.*

Let's just get back to the motorboat, Failure thought, unable to wipe the grin from her sun starved face. *Jada's lads won't follow us past the Tottenham Court dock. No one sets foot in Fitzrovia these days except locals and cons; not even Guzzers.*

But as she rounded a corner onto the cobbled street which would lead to her boat and to safety, Failure skidded to a stop. A thud of horror slammed her in the chest.

It's under water, she gaped. *Greenwich is going under. We'll have to double back.*

Failure felt the usual sting of regret as she turned away. She had always loved the water. It had been easy to stave off loneliness, even in a childhood like Failure's, when there was a sunken kingdom to explore; fishing with her crossbow, knife and net; high diving into the Thames Broad from roofs of sinking skyscrapers; deep diving to pillage the ruins beneath the waves. But all of that had to end. When the Blight had taken hold. And after what had happened that summer to Loss.

Hurrying down a street which branched away from the river, Failure found herself in a maze of market stalls, staying low in the muggy heat.

There were Guzzers patrolling here, armed with crossbows and armoured in their black military uniforms. Turning down a short, narrow passageway, Failure emerged quite suddenly on to a quiet cobbled street. At the far end, a mountain of rolling green parkland rose on a steep incline before her; Greenwich Park. A pair of large iron gates loomed at the dead end of the passageway, hanging at strange angles, overgrown with ivy and glistening brambles, like the entrance to a faery castle.

That's the last place you want to end up, her guts warned. *Especially on the day of the dead.*

I could hide in there, Failure hissed back. *Make a shadow path through the trees like I'm a sneaky forest spirit and get out through one of the exits on the far side.*

But the dead walk in there.

I'm not scared of ghosts, Failure growled back, as the shouts of Jada's lads came closer.

This is a very bad plan, sighed her guts, as Failure gripped the rusted bars and squeezed through the brambles, into the site of old horrors beyond.

The park twitched with a tense bleakness. Small, furtive eyes watched Failure from thickets and briars as she deftly climbed the steep, overgrown paths. The whole park was being suffocated by a crop of superweeds, a second skin of venomous vines and tempting, deadly badberries. Failure had spent many happy hours harvesting these glistening orange fruits, stewing them with seaweed, salt and dates, then decanting the pearlescent orange liquid into a bottle and delivering it to Pa in private. They called it Moonshine. Though Failure thought of it as his Medicine. Pa had dark spells. The Medicine staved them off, but the darkness always came for him in the end. And then you didn't want to be around for a little while.

This park has the shadow on it, Failure's guts warned.

London Undeners are the most superstitious bunch of fools, that's what Pa always says, she whispered back.

Tell that to the congregation of the Royal Observatory Church, her guts sniped. *They were the first to be put to death in this place. Burned inside their own church when they wouldn't kneel to the Kala.*

Well, Failure said with a shudder, as she picked her way over the weeds, *they should have kneeled.*

You sound like Pa, her guts admonished. And they were right. He liked that kind of nasty-ness.

They had had a particularly good morning together, testing Pa's new shipment of weapons on St. Francis Xavier Street. Failure had tied her tangled hair back with a black bandanna and used a precious lump of charcoal to draw camouflage lines across her pale cheeks and black freckles. It had made Pa laugh and clip her round the ear as they wandered down to the vast, gleaming river. Failure had spent a happy hour blasting bottles off brick walls with underwater spear throwers, shooting deadly nightshades with a few decent catapults, and had even speared a rat with a beautiful antique harpoon. Pa had watched her merrily, rocking back on a plastic chair, his bald head and fat bare chest glistening with sweat in the amber glare of the stinking morning oil lamps, laughing uproariously each time Failure had destroyed something. Later, when Failure had brought his lunch up to his office on the second floor of The Townhouse, he had entrusted her with her first ever Task.

You got what you wished for, her guts sighed as they emerged onto a flat expanse at the summit of the park. At the far side stood the blackened red brick shell of the Observatory Church. This had once been a place to observe the constellations. But the smog had smothered the stars long ago, and so the followers of the old Sky God had converted it into a church. Standing before the church, on the grassy plain, were row upon deadly row of crucifix, gallows and pike: a graveyard of torture and execution, abandoned more than a decade ago, back when the resistance had refused to kneel before the Kala. They had left her with no choice. The resistance were rounded up, sacrificed to the Goddess and left for the birds.

There's no such thing as ghosts, Failure told her guts. *Even on the day of the dead.*

Who needs ghosts? her guts murmured.

A flash of movement in the thicket to her side. *One.* Something slinking through the shadows. *Two.* Behind her, carried on the hot acrid wind, that pungent scent of smoked fish. *Three.*

Jada's lads had followed her within. A moment of stillness. And then they broke from their hiding places and ran for her, closing in from all directions at once. Clutching the black box tightly in one arm, Failure sprinted for the Observatory church, crushing poison berries and insects beneath her boots. Scrabbling for the burned doorway, Failure ripped it open and slammed it shut behind herself, fingers finding a cold metal lock and an iron key to turn within it. A moment later the lads collided with the door like a flock of gulls slamming into glass, but the ancient door held fast.

Trying to catch her breath, Failure placed the stolen black box down on the flagstones, ripped the Zeeva crossbow from her back and loaded its three strings with bolts. She looked around for the best escape route. Three walls of the church were solid stone, the fourth was comprised of a vast stained-glass window. As Failure stared at the murky glass images of animals, a boat and angels playing pipes in the sky, a rare ray of violent lemon sunlight pierced the gloom. The stained-glass window burst into a kaleidoscope of colour, bathing Failure in sparkling ruby red, ocean blue and serpent green. She held a hand up before herself, moving it in the swirling shades, feeling like a Time Corp show reel emblazoned on a moving picture screen, waving to adoring crowds.

And there, in the swirling dust, ash and twinkling light, Failure became aware of a steady ticking sound. Just audible in the unnatural quiet. Rapid. More than two beats every single second, tick-tick-tick-tick-tick-tick like the scratch made by a gramophone needle at the end of a song, or like the racing of a frightened heartbeat. Failure had heard the folks in the Townhouse talk about their hearts: being heart-warmed or heavy-hearted, suffering heartache and broken hearts. But Failure knew the true purpose of the heart was to act as an early warning system for danger. People who didn't realise this made themselves vulnerable and slow. But Failure knew and had methodically restricted her own heart from any other work than this purpose; she trusted her guts for everything else. They had made her strong and kept her safe.

The smog shifted once again, extinguishing the spear of light and clamping the sun back into its dark prison. The shimmering screen of colour was switched off, and the usual gloom returned.

That ticking sound is coming from the black box, Failure guts warned her.

It must be a clock or something, Failure replied, kneeling before the box on the cold flagstones. *What a weird thing for Pa to want me to nick.*

There is something else that ticks, her guts quaked. *Something dangerous. And we aren't talking about hearts now.*

Don't be ridiculous, Failure snapped. *Pa would never send us on a Task to nick a goddam bomb. If he really thought there was a bomb in there, he'd have left it in Mumma Dory's Chowder Cafe to take Jada out of the black marketplace.*

And yet, her guts replied.

"Look, I trust him," Failure snapped aloud to the empty church, making herself jump at the sudden sound.

Fine, but maybe this is the wrong box? her guts persisted. *Or what if Jada had somehow got wind that you were coming to nick it, took out the real contents and rigged it up. All ready and raring for you to whisk it away and blow yourself to smithereens.*

Then she wouldn't have sent her sons after me, Failure replied. The unsettling quiet weighed heavily. Where had the lads gone?

Imagine if you turn up at home and present Pa with a bomb that blows both your heads off, her guts mused. *We don't want to go strolling into hell next to that old dog. We'd end up getting sent to the darkest layer of depravity.*

I think I better open the box, Failure sighed.

No choice about that at all, really, her guts replied. *And this genuinely has nothing whatsoever to do with a deep-seated longing to see what's making that lovely tick-tick-tick-tick-tick. That rhythmic beat that sounds like a friend. Sounds like something familiar. Sounds like home.*

Ignoring her guts, Failure used a rock to smash the lock from the metal box. With something akin to a sigh, the box's lid lifted. And there it sat before her. Impatient. Ticking. Bomb.

CHAPTER THREE

I can't believe it, Failure breathed, her mind fogged over with disbelief.

A bomb.

Oh, but you can believe it, her guts retorted without missing a beat. *Because Pa is a gritless drunk with the morals of a bottom feeding shark. And because you're clearly as dispensable to him as anyone else.*

But I'm not, I'm… I'm… But what was she? She was not his child. Not his servant. Not his friend. He had taken her in, after her mother had died on his premises. That was all. *I'm important to him,* she concluded, however unsatisfactorily.

Failure inched towards the bomb and surveyed the mechanism. Within the protective metal shell, a block of dryweed-wrapped gunpower was attached to a common impact fuse and, somewhat bizarrely, also to a small pocket watch timer. When she was about ten years old one of the regulars at the Townhouse's cellar bar had worn a pocket watch in his jacket pocket and made a big show of polishing and winding it.

"He says it's real gold, kiddy," Winston had whispered to Failure, as she poured a rum and bean milk behind the bar. "But it's a piece of tin junk, I tells you that for free." Winston was a sometime lover of Pa's. Tall and thin, with golden brown skin and round spectacles that always slipped down his hooked nose. It was he who had taught Failure to deep dive, before the Blight, and had shown her how to tie a constrictor and a clove hitch. "My mother was a goldsmith, afore the Claiming," Winston had said, "So I know a piece of old painted junk when I see it."

"Why did the Kala Claim all the gold?" Failure had asked.

"For the Time Corp to build their time machines up in the Programmes," Winston had explained. "It's got to be gold. Something to do with electricity. That's why most people gave it all up willingly, you see. Plus, they was the Kala's orders. Keeping it back would've been treason. And you lose more than a hand for treason these days. Harry Fulcher says you stand there in the Courts, getting your Swift Trial done by a judge, and all the while you can hear the screams of the sentences being carried out in the next room." Winston had chuckled and Failure had handed over the rum.

Harry Fulcher's pocket watch might have been tin. But the pocket watch in the bomb was real gold. Unlike the wedding rings and chains and teeth, this watch had somehow escaped the Claiming. Its face was mother of pearl, shimmering with glints of rainbow colours and circled by tiny red rubies. Six small black and white dials were inlaid into it, and the inscription, 'Fortiter ire retro', was engraved on the face in golden lettering. Several tiny knobs poked out at the side, and from the top trailed a long chain. It was the most beautiful thing Failure had ever seen.

A crash sounded against the church's wooden door. The rusted hinges shuddered and creaked but held fast.

Failure snapped the lid of the box shut and tucked it under one arm, sickened by the sensation of a bomb nestled against her ribs. Another crash sounded. Failure grabbed her crossbow and raced to a window on the far side of the church, dragging a wooden bench beneath it. She peeled off her yellow mack and wrapped her fist tight within in, then punched the brittle glass, smashing out the windowpane and rubbing round the edges as Pa had shown her when she was a little girl. Beyond, the park stretched away in darkness. Two people dressed all in black were entering through the distant gates.

Only Guzzers on patrol wear black uniforms like that, Failure's guts told her. *You can't go out there and have them find us with an illegal explosive and a real golden watch! You'll be up before the Swift Courts before you can say Jack-snap-shut!*

Before she could reply, the wooden doorway splintered and with a final bone crunching smash, gave way. Jada's lads streamed within, spreading out into a long line. There were six of them. Failure levelled her crossbow, calling, "Take another step and I'll fire this between your eyeballs."

Failure poised her right forefinger on the first of the three triggers.

"We want that box you nicked from our mother," called Shame, the eldest boy. "You better hand it over or your skin's for the tannery."

"This box belongs to Pa Townhouse," Failure called back, as Shame inched towards her. "Stop moving or I'll slug one of these in you, I swear it."

"It ain't Pa Townhouse's box any more than it's yours, freckle-face," Shame called. "It's Morningside Jack's. And if it ain't back in the Cafe by evening then we're all for it. So, you better hand it over."

"Morningside Jack's?" Failure scoffed. "He's not been seen since the storms in last summer's whaling."

"Guess he's back in town," Shame sneered. "And I tell you what, freckle-face, I don't really care who's box it is. I'm taking it."

Shame ran forwards. Failure fired off all three bolts, hurling herself through the smashed window and falling to the stones beneath with a painful smack.

There's nowhere to run! Failure's guts screamed in her ears, as she sprinted across the grassy plain. *There's Guzzers one way and lads closing in behind us! Pa was right. You weren't clever enough, or quick enough, or brave enough for a Task. We're going to fail. We might never even make it home to disappoint him.*

Stop it! Failure cried, *I've got a plan.*

Oh great, rolled her guts.

You better be a good, big, helluva bomb, Failure told the black box.

I am, I am, I am it ticked beneath her ribs, as Jada's lads streamed out behind her across the super-weed drenched plain.

Failure skidded to a stop and turned to face them. She ripped the lid off the metal box and held it up high. Her breath came in short stabs, hands trembling.

"You want your goddam bomb?" Failure cried, lowering the black metal box slowly to the straw-like grass.

"Whatever you're thinking, just forget it," called Shame, his skin sweating furiously, drips landing on the ground at his feet as he backed away. Failure closed the fingertips of one hand around the block of gunpowder. She scooped the golden pocket watch up with the other. The two came out entirely separately, having never been fixed to one another at all.

"We don't want no bomb. You keep it for yourself, after all, ok?" Shame shouted. "We're gonna go home, now. Don't want no trouble. Gonna tell Mother you ran out of our reach. We'll just let you go, nice and easy. No one'll ever know."

That's a good plan, her guts insisted. *Do what he says. Let them go and we can get out of here in one piece.*

"I know your sort," Failure shouted. "You'd never let me go."

Don't do it, don't do it, screamed her guts. But Failure's mind was set. She drew her right arm back and hurled the explosive through the air. It sailed over the heads of Jada's lads, who watched it arc above them. Then, with a tinkling sound, it smashed through the stained-glass window. There was a moment of suspended nothingness as the unseen bomb plummeted towards the unseen stone floor within. Jada's lads scattered, as Failure turned on her heel and began to flee as fast as her being would carry her. And then came an almighty, blood shaking 'BOOOOOM'. Failure was lifted off her feet and slammed into the hard earth and badberry weed. Dirt kicked up into her eyes and mouth. The air was knocked from her lungs. Her ears screamed with a shrill ringing.

Lying on her stomach, Failure spat dirt and dust, feeling a thrill of success for a single sweet, hot moment. But then a crunching and moaning sounded from somewhere behind her, a grinding of brick and glass. The ancient structure and its ghosts screamed as the building collapsed and the stained-glass wall began to fall outwards. Failure lay beneath the toppling mass. Under the weight of red brick and black tiles and stained glass and ancient mortar, she would be crushed. Five seconds 'til death.

"I wanted to live, and I want you to stop, just for a moment, just a moment or two, please. Wait!" Failure reached her arms forwards, one hand still pointlessly gripping the pocket watch and its dangling chain. "Please, WAIT!"

A white heat erupted across Failure's skin. It hissed through her like an icy wave. And then it was gone. The world stood perfectly still. Inches above Failure's head, thousands of shards of rainbow glass sparkled and glistened. Suspended in the rare winter dusk sunlight. Motionless. Everything still as stone. The fleeing lads. Every strand of grass. Even the breeze. Everything held perfectly still. Failure managed to draw a shuddering breath into her winded lungs.

What are you waiting for?! screamed her guts. *Get away from under this wall of arrows you goddam fool! Run!*

Failure leapt to her feet. She raced out from under the frozen, falling wall of rainbow arrows and across the grassland of the park. When she reached the dark of the treeline, there was a terrible lurch in her stomach. Failure stumbled and landed hard on hands and knees. The world around her became alive once more and, with a tremendous crunching and crashing, the church completed its descent to the earth, shaking the very ground beneath her.

What were you thinking? her guts screamed as Failure raced for a shaded exit, fleeing down the steep hill on a deserted, cracked tarmac road. *You threw a bomb! Threw it! Don't you care if you die?! That was the worst plan anyone has ever had!*

I can't really believe it worked either, Failure laughed, as she came to the breezy river's edge.

A large motorboat was bobbing at a small jetty. It was black, emblazoned with the golden ivy and anchor symbol of the Time

Corp, and was very likely the boat belonging to the pair of Guzzers from the park.

Realising that it was still in her hand, Failure shoved the golden pocket watch into her yellow mac pocket. She stepped into the motorboat, kicking the engine open and hot-wiring it to life. As the boat purred happily into being, Failure steered it out onto the vast breadth of the Thames Broad, and with the cool spray of poisoned salt water on her skin, turned her thoughts toward The Townhouse and the wrath of Pa.

CHAPTER FOUR

What's Pa gonna say when he finds out you exploded the bomb? her guts churned, as Failure steered the stolen motorboat into Fitzrovia.

I don't care what he's got to say, Failure fumed, scraping the day's smog grit from her eyes and nose. *I want to give him a piece of my mind.*

The black Edwardian whale oil lamps which lined the Fitzrovia streets, were burning their pungent honey yellow fuel in the afternoon gloom as Failure secured the motorboat at Pa's private jetty. She instructed the afternoon watchman to consider the boat a part of Pa's fleet, then headed for home.

The Townhouse. Once an elegant white mansion, years of smog grits had smeared its balconies and pillars with a slick grey fur, and the roof was reinforced against the rains and fire storms with ugly corrugated iron sheets. It had functioned for decades as a market, social club and hunting ground for the ne'er-do-wells and neverspeaks of the whole northern bank of London Under. It was the only home Failure had known. She had manned the smoky basement bar and fetched and carried in the role of not-quite-adopted-child, servant, hanger-on and slave for Pa and his various partners over the years.

She had grown up amongst the women and men who made their living renting rooms, selling and trading over the Townhouse's five floors. By the time she was eight years old, Failure was no stranger to the scent of opium, the cries of birthing pain, the magic of cards and crystals; by the time she was ten she could list the black market prices for any boat, weapon, drug or fuel in town, and on her eleventh Winter Solstice she was given her first crossbow.

There had been Edmund, who was sharp tongued with most, but seemed to enjoy having Failure chattering away in his sewing shop on the ground floor. There had been Blanche, who taught her to hunt with a bow and arrow and a crossbow, but who didn't stay long. And McGuvvorn, who had run an arms trade from the second floor, and who had taught Failure how to read. He had got into a dispute in the bar one night and was found hanging by the feet above the river, his head beneath the waves. That sort of end wasn't unknown amongst the clients and the traders of The Townhouse, but Failure missed Winston the most. Of all Pa's partners over the years, he had stayed the longest. But Winston had long since moved on, like everyone moved on in the end. Except Failure.

We've always been alright here, she said to her guts, as she hurried up the broad stone steps.

We've always been busy here, her guts corrected. *Maybe that's the same thing.*

The doorman opened the large black door without a word and Failure crossed under the dusty chandelier in the grand entrance lobby, racing up the red carpeted staircase directly to Pa's office. She hammered on the dark wood and called, "It's me, I'm back."

"Come in," came a gravelly voice from within. "It's open." She heard the edge of darkness in him.

Inside the office, The Kala smiled down regally from a life size portrait behind the desk, dramatic in her red military suit and medals, with her long, plaited grey hair and brass sceptre. Pa's three treasured electric eels glared suspiciously with their tiny blue eyes, swimming in the saltwater tank atop the desk like dark grey snakes. Pa sat in an armchair by the open window, one foot hooked up on the window ledge. He wore his usual cream-coloured jeans, round stomach bulging over his belt, a fat silver chain hanging over his bare chest amidst the sparce covering of white hair. As Failure stepped within and closed the door, he sipped a glass of pearly, orange-coloured moonshine and stared at her.

"Where's my black box, kiddy?"

"Did you see me coming in to the jetty, m'love?" Failure stalled, gesturing to the view of the river from the window. The black waves were lapping Pa's little fleet in the amber lamp light. "Saw I upgraded your boat? That one's a genuine Guzzer motorboat. Cuts the waves like butter. Lick of paint and she's good as gold."

"Nice try. Where's my black box, kiddy?" He asked again.

"There was a goddam bomb in that box," Failure cried. "I was hurling it around London Under all afternoon like a sack of potatoes. It should've killed me! And you should've warned me!"

"You've wanted a Task for years, Fey," Pa said in his ice-cool blankness. "If you think you're too special to be sent out for something dangerous then I done you a disservice. Given you delusions of grandeur. Made you weak."

"I'm not goddam weak," Failure spat back. "But you should've give me the full picture, not sent me on a suicide mission."

"You're alive and well enough to be making a hellcat noise right here and now," Pa growled, shifting the heavy silver chain on his chest and wiping away a sheen of sweat. "And you know better than to moan at me when a storm's coming. Sit down."

Failure sat.

"You, in your little kid shorts and your silly yellow mac," he said, a smile twitching at the corner of his lips. "Not quite beautiful like your mother. Feh-lih-sih-teeee. She had bright yellow hair, long, like yours, but sort of curly and soft, like living gold. Your eyes came out pale brown, when hers were almost green, especially in firefly light. Her skin was as white as snow. She wasn't just sun-starved like the rest of us, she was already meant to be pale. And goddess, she had a wicked laugh. She was just a little bit slightly mad. Wild in her eyes, she was. Dangerous. Bewitching. Drank like a nightwalker. Swore like an old East End mobster. Laughed like a sailor. She would've found this hilarious. We would've laughed. Goddess I miss her. She even laughed when she died. So they say. You ain't come out wild like her, Fey."

"Yeah, well maybe I'll live a bit longer than she did," Failure said in a small, fierce voice, glaring at him without humour.

"Yeah, there's salt grit in you, the likes of which she never had. Only just coming up to the surface. Now where's my black box?"

"I chucked it and it blew up a church," Failure replied. There was a moment of intense silence before Pa began to laugh uproariously. And there was something strange behind his laughter. It wasn't anger. He was angry most of the time. But that manifested as a bubbling, seething fury or a screaming, spitting violence. This was something new.

He fell silent and stared at her with his narrow, ice blue eyes. "So, you not only lost the bomb," he said in a low voice, "you deployed the bomb. You alerted the attention of half of London-bleeding-Under. You've lived up to your name today, Failure. I can't have that. People have to know – whoever you are – that you can't fail me." He glanced, just for a moment, at his weapons collection, concealed behind the false wall of the bookshelf to his right.

Failure's heart pounded a warning and she readied herself to run for it. She knew the deadly contents of that concealed cabinet. She had polished it all often enough; harps, bows, clubs, all manner of killing machines. And of course Pa's personal quirk for antique weaponry of the old days; grenades, swords and knives. But instead of going to the concealed weapons cabinet, Pa crossed to his desk, fishing for something at the back of a draw.

Give him the pocket watch now, her guts urged her. *A treasure will make a success of the failed Task. Pa can flog it for the gold alone.*

Pa tossed a snakeskin wallet onto the desk, then crossed back to the windows. He stared out into the dusk. "I've always been good to you, haven't I?" he said quietly, his sudden change of tone making Failure prickle. "And you know what happened to her – your mother – do you?" There was a doubtful gleam in his pale blue eyes. In that gleam, Failure saw the shadow of a thousand drunken conversations, after which he had no memory of what he had told her.

"Yeah, I know about it," Failure told him, her small, pointed chin raised defiantly against the world. "You got Winston to tell me on my ninth Winter Solstice. We were eating strawberry jam sponge in the bar and you made him tell me everything. Said I should know, now I was armed. I couldn't never stand the taste of jam sponge any more after that. Why're you talking about her?"

"That wallet has a letter in it," Pa said. "From your mother. You might as well have it, now. Damn you, Fey."

His words jumbled and thumped in her guts. A letter. From her mother. She took the snakeskin wallet and slipped it into her jeans pocket before he could change his mind.

Pa's eyes were watering as he took a long drink of moonshine. "You'll always be a kid to me, Fey. However old the world lets you get to be. Always be a funny kid to me. It's the biggest regret of my life, you know."

"The letter? Or the bomb?" Failure asked. But Pa only chuckled.

A speedboat had docked on the riverbank beside the stolen motorboat and the evening watchman was lying motionless on the jetty. Two Guards were trooping towards The Townhouse, helmet visors down and harpoons in hand. One of them was dragging the eldest of Jada's lads, Shame, along with them. They were the Guzzers from the park. And they had followed her all the way into goddam Fitzrovia.

Shame pointed up at The Townhouse from the street below. The Guzzer released him and he fled like a bolt from a bow.

"Biggest regret of my life, hands down," Pa repeated in a wistful voice. "After all these years. Having to let you go." He plunged one hand into the fish tank on his desk, drawing out the thick, gleaming body of an eel. Failure leapt back, reaching for her bow and realising that it was buried under hundreds of tonnes of rubble in Greenwich Park. She ducked as Pa flung the eel's rubbery body at her neck and missed her by an inch. Roaring in rage, Failure kicked out for his knee with a right boot, but he had taught her everything she had ever known, and anticipated the attack, stepping aside. Overbalancing, Failure fell with a crash to the floor. Pa stood above her and dropped the eel like a graveyard shovel. Before she could raise a hand to protest, the ravenous creature had wrapped itself around her neck, completing its circuit and delivering its electric charge into her spine.

CHAPTER FIVE

Failure's eyes flickered open, pain stabbing the back of her skull and neck. She was lying in an inch of water on the deck of a large speedboat, thrumming over the waves of the Thames Broad. The water had woken her, inconstant old friend as it was. The night itself was black as treacle, the air sticky, clammy and heavy with the oncoming storm.

Why in the goddam are we out on the open water when a storm's due? whispered her guts.

These two must be careless, green, or out of their minds, Failure murmured back.

They look like Guzz, her guts churned.

But they aren't, Failure replied. *There's no golden crest on their jackets. And those are military grade harpoons. So are their helmets. Has Pa handed us over to the goddam secret police?*

Treacherous, cowardly con, her guts clenched. *Gave us over as quick and easy as a guillotine slicing through a neck.*

Failure glared at the starless black curtain of night and silently swore, *I will reap a terrible revenge on that scab. You can witness that.*

You're sailing East, the sky breathed down colourlessly from above.

Whitechapel, the pocket watch ticked with dismay. *You're being taken to the Courts of Swift Justice.*

The Kala's Judges passed sentences which were carried out immediately in the adjoining rooms; be that a whipping, an execution, or any of the horrors in between. You lost a hand for thieving. She'd seen poor dead Harry Fulcher's remaining stump a couple of months before. He'd been sat at the bar, ranting and angry, full of pain and fury, and Failure had served him the Townhouse's speciality; a dirty pint laced with opium, for four thousand quid. He was still handsome, with his long dark hair and blue eyes, but the oozing bandages made him stink, despite the lavender tied around his neck, and the women didn't flock around him anymore. He'd been dead within the week, and no one had replaced him in room seven ever since. Superstitious bunch, London Undeners.

You've got to escape before they get you into the Courts, her guts insisted. *Or we'll be under lock, key and guillotine before you can say Jack-snap-shut. You didn't just nick government supplies of petrol. You blew up a church.*

Failure surveyed her two captors. The eldest had long white hair tied in a low ponytail and a thick scar across his lip and cheek. The other was barely older than Failure, almost certainly still in his conscription years. Pa had been adamant that Failure would never face the conscription at eighteen like the others. "No kid like you should be serving with the Guzzers or the army, Fey," he had always said. "Right now they don't know you exist, so we'll keep it that way." To this end, Failure had never attended a school, and never been permitted to mix with anyone outside of the relative safety of Fitzrovia.

The younger officer was manning the helm. He had skin the colour of black coffee and hair that was turning silver despite his youth. He was far over six feet tall and impossibly muscular. Failure would never in a million years be able to overpower him.

"Get up and get yourself comfortable," the older officer with the white hair said. "How's your head?"

"Like I was blasted with 500 volts in the brain by a scumbag with an eel," Failure replied as she clambered up and onto one of the benches. "How's yours?"

"Keep your voice down," the officer replied. "We're taking you to Major Atsila. Won't be long."

Major Atsila must be a Judge in the Courts, hissed Failure's guts.

Isn't it only Barons who sit in the Courts? the pocket watch asked.

It's not gonna make much difference who hears the case though is it? Failure thought, darkly. A flash of light caught her eye; a golden, wobbling, inconsistent thing under the water. She looked away.

"I'm gonna find and kill that traitor," Failure said as they approached the sinking remains of the old Tower Bridge. "Maybe I'll kill your Major Atsiler too," she added. "I'm good with bows and clubs. Got any spare?"

The face of the young man at the helm creased into a hidden smile. It faded, however, as they passed between the remains of the old bridge. The triangular tips and blue battlements poked up from the middle of the river, decorated with rotting body parts and putrid severed heads. A silent warning to the city dwellers from the Kala and her Barons. Dozens of vultures plucked and picked at the feast, unconcerned by the approaching vessel.

"Do their ghosts come visiting you?" Failure asked the young officer at the helm.

"Excuse me?" He asked.

"The ghosts of the convicts. On the Pillars. I'm guessing you lot sent some of them to their deaths. Do they come and visit you? Especially on Samhain, being the festival of the dead and all that. We look away, in London Under, when we go haunted places. Or if there's stuff in the water. Look away and they can't follow you."

"I don't believe in ghosts or monsters," the young man replied.

"More fool you, then, m'love," Failure said.

"We are on the Thames Broad at night," the senior officer barked. "Keep quiet and keep your wits switched on. Smith, focus on the driving. Twenty minutes, no more."

"But we're almost at the Courts now," Failure hissed. "Don't you know where you're going?"

"We aren't taking you to the Courts," the younger officer told

28

her, "The Commander already said; we're going to Crossness to see Major Atsiler. The water's getting choppy, Sir."

"We'll give it another minute," the Commander said, his scarred face crumpling into a frown.

"Pardon, Sir," Smith went on, quiet but firm. "We were briefed to be very cautious of a sudden change in the water."

"We were also briefed to get the target directly to the rendezvous and deliver," the Commander said. "We'll try and stay on track."

"We can only deliver the goods if we don't drown the goods on route," Smith insisted.

"You won't be drowning in a fire storm," Failure grinned. "No one drowns. They burn."

"We stay on track," the Commander insisted. But as he spoke, the stillness of the evening air was ripped open by a sudden loud flapping of wings. The vultures were fleeing their feast on Tower Bridge.

"Alright, we can't risk it, get us to the bank, Smith" the Commander cried, slamming down the visor on his black helmet.

Far up in the smog thickened sky, amber lights were appearing, vivid orange stars picking their way down through the smog. But these weren't stars. They were burning orange and yellow flames. The storm had come at last. The first of the flames rained down, mesmerising and flickering like fireworks. Failure pulled the hood of her yellow rain mac over her head and tucked her bare knees inside, dusting herself free of sparks.

The flaming, falling stars came thicker and faster, burning their way through the smog with a hiss and wheezing down to extinguish in the water. When one of the falling stars landed on a building across the river, it fizzed up in a sudden inferno of all consuming fire. Soon the air around them was full of sparking, hissing orange flames. Failure wondered now at the peculiar beauty of it.

"Grab yourself a helmet from under the bench," the Commander shouted to Failure through a crackling speaker on his helmet. Failure clambered down onto the damp deck and reached under the bench. Her fingers felt for the roundness of the helmet but collided with something cold and metallic instead.

That's a harpoon, gasped her guts. *Grab it!* She closed her fingers around the cold metal and drew it silently into the quiet shadow of her yellow mac, then grabbed one of the heavy black helmets. As she squeezed the tight, black foam interior onto her head, Failure's world became muffled and dark. She slipped the visor up, so as to see more easily, but the commander reached across and slammed it back down. Failure went to protest, but at that moment the boat smacked into a rickety jetty with a grinding crunch. A flare of vivid red lightening rent through the blackness, filling the void between smog and river, a momentary scarlet scar in the darkness. Deafening thunder roared. Smith grabbed Failure by her upper arm and dragged her out of the boat.

On the deserted street ahead, gas lamps burned in the windows of an old-fashioned London pub, who's faded sign swung madly in the hot wind. The walls had long ago been pasted with posters of a handsome blonde haired young man, stood with legs apart, one hand on his hip, the other raising a forefinger to the sky. "Reckless O'Neil, the Kala salutes you! Go bravely in the past!"

Another terrific flash of red lightening lit up the night, and a building several streets away exploded into vicious flames. Bone shaking thunder roared in the unfathomable sky above, as the Commander hammered on the pub door, shouting, "Commanding Officer claiming sanctuary in the name of the Kala. Open up! Smith, get ready to smash this door down."

Now's your chance, whilst they're distracted, hissed Failure's guts. Carefully drawing the harpoon out from under her mac, Failure backed down the stone steps, shouting, "Don't move, either of you. I've got all four triggers loaded and I'll mincemeat you if you flinch for your harps."

"What're you doing? The Commander called angrily. "Get out of the storm, you fool,"

"I'll take my chances," Failure called back. "I've known enough ne'er-do-wells and neverspeaks to know all about what happens in the Courts of Swift Justice."

"We told you; we're not taking you to the Courts," the Commander barked back. "We're taking you to a Recruiter called Major Atsila at Crossness."

"Shut up and lay your weapons down," Failed shouted.

"You don't understand what's going on here," Smith called angrily, keeping a firm grip on his harp.

"Just do it," the Commander barked and, looking as though it cost him a great fortune, Smith also placed his harp on the ground.

"You need to let us explain," the Commander's voice called over the crackle and roar of the storm. He found Failure's gaze through the falling orange sparks. "Keep the harpoon levelled at us the whole time if you have to, just please get inside. You have to trust us."

"I don't trust anyone," Failure replied. And she raised the visor of her helmet. As the fresh air hit her face, Failure was met with a scent. It was carried to her on the hot wind; stinking, rotten flesh and hair. Musky and bloody and salty and stale. A dark sliver of movement flickered in the darkness. A plume of steamy breath. A flash of glowing amber light. The storm had woken it. It was close. It had hunted them from the water. Had them in its sights. One of the river Sylkies. It would rip the officers to shredded meat on the slabs.

The Sylkie emerged behind the officers. It was young, less than a year at most. But it was a sleek, ugly killing machine all the same. Its muscular body was covered in peeling dark scale, stinking and rotten. It moved low to the ground in the manner of an alligator, though its long legs gave it the prowl of a jungle cat. Its wide grin showed two rows of small, sharp teeth barred in a muzzle that sniffed and puffed in the storm; thick yellow saliva dripping from its teeth.

You make a run for it while the Sylkie attacks them. Sneak away into the stormy night.

The commander gave you the helmet to protect you, the pocket watch raced disapprovingly. *And the big guy secretly thought you were funny.*

Pa would say we should leave them out here as Sylkie food and get to goddam safety, Failure's guts insisted.

Pa, who sent you on a suicide mission? the watch ticked back. *Pa, who handed you over to the Secret Police? And you know what else he did. Long ago.*

This is your only chance to escape, her guts fought back.

But if that Sylkie eats them alive... Failure worried. *Then that's not a good death. It would bring the shadow on me.*

Then you're going to have to give away your advantage, her guts laughed. *You'll probably get gobbled up by the Sylkie before you even have a chance to be recaptured and executed for your crimes. Pa would say you were a bleeding hearted idiot.*

A wicked smile spread over Failure's pale, black-freckled face, as she replied, *Yeah, well I'm not working for him anymore.*

CHAPTER SIX

Failure licked the sticky, hot ash from her green-tinged lips, tasting a rank, metallic twang. She whispered her own name, "Failure." The lamp-like eyes of the Sylkie snapped across to her in the dark. They fixed on her.

You're of the storm, she mused silently, holding the Sylkie's gaze. *And so am I.* Her finger felt fragile against the cool trigger.

"Get down!" Failure screamed into the night. The younger officer dropped to the ground with military precision. But the Commander took a deadly moment to glance behind and screamed in horror at the monster before him. A flash of amber, a shimmer of gold fur and black scales in the rain. The Sylkie was on him. Growling and screaming rent the night air.

Failure fired all four of her bolts at the back of the creature, which howled in rage and reared on its hind legs. Red lightning flashed overhead and with a tremendous, deafening roar, the smog clouds themselves burst into flame. Now the sky burned bright as a summer's day in a distant land. Smith, lit orange in the fierce glow, grabbed for his weapon and the Sylkie thudded back down onto four paws, batting a burning ember from its ear with a paw. Bolts flew and the creature roared again, then pounded over the Commander's body towards them.

In a blinding flurry of falling fire, burning rain, slicing claws and the tat-tat-tat of harpoon bolts, Failure could only hurl the stolen harpoon at the Sylkie, which bounced off its armoured flesh. Smith pounced forward as the creature raised a great clawed paw at him, then sent a bolt flying at the creature's face. Roaring in fury, the Sylkie took the bolt down its throat. A second bolt was fired and met with one glowing yellow eye, and the brain matter behind. The Sylkie jerked like a fish on a line, before slumping to the ground, dead as a sack of shells.

Failure panted to regain her breath, as the smog clouds above puttered out and the last of the falling flames hissed to nothingness on the paving at her feet. The night was plunged back into darkness. The storm had burned itself out.

"Are you ok?" Smith called to Failure as he ran towards the motionless body of the Commander.

Yes, get the weapon and get the goddam out of here, her guts advised.

Weapon, then boat, Failure agreed and began searching for a glint of metal in the darkness.

"You saved us," Smith called as he leaned over the Commander. "Getting rounds into that thing early on. Good job you're not a bad shot with a harp."

"Maybe I am a bad shot," Failure called back. "Maybe I was aiming for you."

"Either way, you saved us. Well, you saved two of us," he added grimly. "The Commander's dead."

A low growl sounded in the darkness. Deep and slow and resonant. It came from the throat of the dead creature. Which began to stir. The bolts, which had been so violently lodged in its throat and eye and brain, lay on the flagstones like driftwood, washed up in a pool of oily black blood.

"Mother Goddess," Smith breathed. "It's alive. How can it be alive?"

Failure turned on her heel and ran. Smith followed hot on her heels. Glancing back, she saw the Sylkie climbing to its feet, shoulder blades slinking beneath its scales as it followed them.

Failure reached the boat first, leaping in and kicking the engine into life. Smith tore the rope from the mooring and leapt aboard just as Failure floored the acceleration. The Sylkie skidded to a halt before the water, slashing after them with a broad paw and missing Smith's silver-haired head by a whisper.

As they sped away, the shadowed figure watched them go. The eye which had taken the harp bolt was streaming with glutinous black tears, streaked through with rainbow colours like petrol. But it was whole. It had healed. The Sylkie looked away, licking blood splatters from the pavement with a rough, pink tongue. Then it slunk down the bank and into the water, vanishing beneath the waves.

"It's gone into the water," Failure told Smith, as he took the helm and she climbed over to a bench, sticky with rain. "So make this thing move fast."

"Gone into the water?" Smith asked from the other side of the boat. "How could it?"

"Just don't go moon bathing any time soon," Failure replied. "That was a young one. The big ones might be down there with it."

"Why in the hells did you try and run away?" Smith asked, still breathless.

"You think I'm just gonna go along quietly with the Secret Police to get my legs sawn off or Jack-snap-whatever at the courts?"

"You think we're the secret police?" Smith asked. "They don't go around in uniform. You wouldn't know Secret Police from your best friend or your own mother."

Tell him you don't have either of those things, her guts suggested, unhelpfully.

"We're with a branch of the military," Smith went on. "I already told you; we were taking you to meet with Major Atsiler."

"I never heard of no-one called Atsiler," Failure muttered.

"She's a Recruiter," Smith explained.

"What's the army need recruiters for?" Failure asked him, eyes narrowing. "Everyone's got their five years conscription at eighteen, haven't they? Who needs recruiting?"

"She's not a recruiter for the military," Smith replied, scanning the dark river ahead. "She works for the Time Programmes."

CHAPTER SEVEN

"So, I'm not your prisoner?" Failure asked, a swooping sensation in her stomach, a white nothingness in her mind.

"No…" Smith replied, slowly. "But Major Atsiler wants to see you. So, she'll see you."

"What if I don't want to be seen?"

"Why would you not want to be seen?" Smith retorted. "She hasn't recruited from London Under before. Unsurprisingly. This town is poison."

"Only if you don't know what you're doing," Failure replied, surprised by how protective she felt of her filthy, remorseless, violent home.

"Well, Atsiler obviously thinks it has promise," Smith said. "Otherwise, she wouldn't consider it as a location. That's what we were here to scout out."

Failure watched the riverbanks stretch impossibly far apart from one another, as the boat sailed along the estuary and out towards the open sea. A thick, silvery mist was settling on everything it touched, glowing brightly despite the pitch-black night.

"I don't like the look of this stuff," Smith said quietly. "Any idea what it is?"

"Don't you get mists after fire storms where you're from?" Failure asked.

"We don't get fire storms," he corrected.

"Just try not to breathe it in," Failure advised. "And don't touch it."

"Why not?"

"Bad for you," Failure replied. "Look, I don't even know what this 'selection' thing is that you're on about. And I don't give a goddam and I don't want nothing to do with it."

"How do you not know about the selection?" Smith asked. "Haven't you been training for it in school?"

Failure scrambled in her mind for some way of excusing her absence from school, but only found the words, "All I want is to get off the goddam Thames Broad before there's another storm. You clearly don't know what you're doing."

"Selection is the process that kids go through in order to get into the Time Programmes," Smith explained. "It's a whole year of testing; physical, mental, spiritual. To find the elite, the gifted, the strong, the ones who could cope with it all. It's exhausting. Brutal."

"Sounds great," Failure muttered.

"Major Atsiler meets a lot of kids," he went on. "Only a tiny fraction of them even get into the selection. Of course, if you do make it, it can open some impressive doors for your future," Smith went on quietly over the hum of the speedboat. "Take me as an example. I arrived in Bristol Bay on a steamer with nothing but a bag of clothes and the four thousand pounds my mother had in her wallet. Refugees, when Lastland went under. Almost had to give ourselves in to the slavers in Bristol Bay. More than once. But then I got into selection. If you're dropped from selection, which I was, you're still considered extremely worthwhile goods. A lot of the kids are picked up by the military, officer training or the Guard, and avoid conscription altogether. I went straight into Atsiler's recruitment team for the Royal Scottish Programme. Something like that could happen for you. You might not even have to do conscription at all."

And no burnt skin and missing toes picking cockles and scrap from the Thames Broad mud flats, mused the pocket watch hidden in Failure's jeans.

Hmmm, her guts mused back. *The old ticker has a point.*

"It's Royal Scots that you'd be considered for," Smith went on, his face radiant with pride. "And assuming that you don't know much about it, The Royal Scottish Programme has been the leading light of the Time Corp for a decade. All six kids who've Travelled studied at Royal Scots. Imagine that."

From out of the gathering mist, rose a huge, ramshackle marina. Dozens of boats, bobbing like giant gulls on the water. The wind sliced through towering masts and wires, making a strangled, whining sound, along with the persistent clanging of metal cables; a tuneless song of the sea. Many of the smaller boats were in good repair; clippers, row boats, kayaks and dinghies. But the larger boats were sitting in the water at awkward angles, their hulls rotting. Amongst all this was a spectacular white yacht. She was enormous and elegant, her shape reminiscent of the narrow, pointed grace of a shark. Oil lamps flickered in her many windows and "The Sorrow" was painted across her body in golden lettering. There were more than a dozen officers stood to attention on the decks and at the gangplank, all of them armed with military issue harps.

"Mind your manners with Major Atsiler, ok?" Smith advised Failure as they pulled up at the mooring. "Try not to be so… you know, like… yourself," he added, and again Failure saw a glint of laughter beneath the formal exterior.

Could we run for it? she asked her guts.

Not a chance, they sighed back, as exhaustion settled on Failure, dense as the gathering silver mist at her feet.

Failure followed Smith up a creaking gangplank and onto the broad beach deck. An imposing woman stood before them, and as the pair approached she released a messenger pigeon up into the starless sky and watched it soar away to the North. She had a long, straight nose and high cheekbones. One of her eyes was concealed behind a neat black eye patch and her long black hair was brightly streaked with grey. She wore shining patent black shoes and a navy-blue military trouser suit, which bore several colourful medals, and the brass Anchor and Ivy of the Time Corp.

"Good evening, Smith," said the woman. "Just the two of you?"

"The Commander was mortally injured during the journey here, Ma'am," Smith replied. "The circumstances were unfavourable to recovering his body, but I was able to collect his personal items before assuming command."

"Understood," the woman replied. "And this is the girl?"

"This is her," Smith replied.

"What do you shoulder for the Goddess?" the woman asked, her one visible eye piercing and pale green, like a marble.

"I shoulder the Failure."

"A pleasure to meet you, Failure. I am Major Dyani Atsiler, Senior Recruiting Officer for the Royal Scottish Time Programme. Is there anyone we should alert that you're here and safe?"

Failure shook her head.

"Very well. We weren't here on recruiting work, not least because the upcoming selection process is already oversubscribed. So, you are a surprise to us. But you look like you are ready to collapse with exhaustion, which is unsurprising given the… unusual events of the day. Why don't you go and have a buttered raisin bun and a hot cocoa in your cabin. Then get some sleep and we can worry about the rest in the morning? Smith, cabin twelve, please." Atsiler waved a hand at Smith and stalked away. The offer of shelter, food and drink made Failure's limbs dissolve into sacks of flour. The back of her neck, where the eel had delivered its shock, began to throb and burn, in response to the hope of rest and repair.

Smith led Failure through a pair of glass doors into a reception with a grand, carpeted staircase. At the summit, a young man emerged and stood peering down. A sliver of mist breathed inside through the open doors and swirled slowly up the staircase toward him. He wore jeans and a dark blue sweatshirt, the hood pulled up over his head, from which a few whisps of wavy, bark-brown hair strayed. In his arms he held a velvety grey rabbit.

The young man stepped down into the mist; feet, then hips, then chest. As they passed one another, Failure's arm brushed against his. His skin was kissed brown by sun from a distant place, free of smog. His eyes were the colour of a conker cracked fresh from the shell. Failure's heart quickened its early warning in her chest, as though it wanted to beat a path up her throat and choke her there.

We've met with some unrivalled danger in this place, haven't we? her guts burned.

We have.

Failure watched the boy exit through the glass doors and walk out onto the deck. He lifted the rabbit up in his hands, then made a violent twist to snap the creature's neck. It hung limply in its own warm grey skin, a dead rock in a sack. He threw the body into the silver mist of the deck. With a heavy flutter of wings, a large, ugly white bird landed with a slam onto the body of the rabbit. It buried its yellow beak and face into the warm flesh and began to feast. The boy crouched beside the great ugly bird, stroking its white feathers as they slowly soaked pink with blood.

CHAPTER EIGHT

Failure woke the next morning as though falling from a great height. She froze. Instantly fearful. She was laid, fully dressed, where she had collapsed on a bed in Cabin Twelve the night before.

"I'll leave you to it," Smith had said quietly at the door. "Someone will be outside all night. If you need anything, just call out."

Look at us, her guts had murmured as she rolled on the silken bedsheets and white fur blanket. *If only Pa could see us now.*

Yeah, she had sighed back, longing for the tiny, stuffy attic room of home, where she suddenly understood she would never sleep again. *Who even knew places like this still existed in the drowning world?*

She had hidden the golden pocket watch and the snakeskin wallet inside her yellow mac and fallen into oblivion.

Now, climbing off the bed, she hung the golden pocket watch safely around her neck. Its beautiful mother-of-pearl face, ruby rim and golden lettering glinting at her, the tick-tick-tick-tick-tick-tick of its innards reassuring against her skin. The snakeskin wallet she went to stow in the back pocket of her jeans. But first Failure paused. She unzipped it, peering inside. The papyrus it contained was yellow with age.

What do you think it says? Wondered her guts.

I dunno, Failure replied with an unusual heaviness.

Well, there's only one way to find out, the pocket watch ticked. *You have to read it.*

But a knock sounded at the door and Failure pocketed the wallet, opening the door to Smith, who was immaculate in a clean uniform.

"You look a lot nicer when you aren't kidnapping people or covered in blood and guts," Failure told him.

"Thank you," he smiled. "So do you. Major Atsiler would like to see you for breakfast."

"How do you like your cabin?" Atsiler asked, as Smith led Failure into a plush lounge on the top floor of the yacht.

"It's ok," Failure shrugged.

"Why don't you come over and sit with me here?" Atsiler gestured to the grand table in the centre of the room. "We can have a bite to eat and a chat."

A large silver platter, covered with a stiff, gleaming white cloth sat between them. When the Major whipped the cloth away, she revealed a feast of fresh green apples, shining red tomatoes on the vine, fluffy white buns of bread filled with raisins and cherries, gleaming butter, olives, nuts, folds of smoked salmon and fillets of smoked mackerel. There was also a thick juice which looked a little like moonshine but turned out to be freshly squeezed orange. Failure dived into the salty, sweet, ripe delicious feast with fingers stained green by lichen tox.

"How are you feeling today?" the Major asked.

"Glad I'm not dead," Failure replied through a mouthful.

"Yes, I have been told about the... the unorthodox measures that your friend took when transferring you to my officers," the Major said with a frown.

"Oh, the electric eel thing?" Failure asked. "No, I meant escaping from the Sylkie that tried to rip us to shreds."

"Sylkie?" The Major asked.

"You know, the monster that attacked me and your men. We call them Sylkies round here. What d'you call them?"

"I think we would be wise to use the term 'creature' rather than, 'monster' or 'Sylkie' in referencing that incident. Smith has reported that you were an asset. Very impressive. He also reported an incident in the park yesterday. He saw something that resembled a time mirage appear in the atmosphere following a vast explosion. You were very close by at the time."

Failure remembered every fraction of every second, from the hungry expressions of Jada's lads and boom of the bomb to the frozen glass wall above her, and the single strands of grass, frozen still.

"I remember the explosion," she replied. "But I dunno about some time mirage. I dunno what one is."

"I see. Well, Failure, I believe that you may have talents, perhaps untapped at this time, which would be of interest to the ongoing war against Time. How old are you?"

"Sixteen last winter solstice."

"Born on winter solstice day?" Atsiler asked, with a raised eyebrow.

"I guess so," Failure frowned. "But I dunno if that's really my birthday."

"And the man who gave you the electric shock?"

"He was sort of my boss," Failure told her. "But I'm not gonna be working for him anymore."

"I see. And what do you know about the Time Programmes?"

"Well," Failure frowned, crunching a mouthful of bread and butter. "I know the Time Corp is sending kids back in time to try and stop the floods. Before there's no land left to live on. And the Time Programmes is where they train them up."

"That's right. And why do we need to stop the floods?"

"Cos the water got poisoned by the Great Quake," Failure replied. "And it's getting worse every year."

"And what do you know about the Great Quake?"

"Big old earthquake," Failure sighed. "Happened in the Arctic. The floods got a lot worse afterwards, and the water got poisoned. And there were fires and droughts and all the goddam drama you like, m'love. They call it the Devastation."

"Very good. What have you asked the Goddess for, in your prayers, Failure?" Major Atsiler asked, staring across with a steely gaze.

"A comfy bed on a super yacht," Failure replied with a twisted grin.

"Do you know the origins of Goddess worship?" Atsiler pressed, leaning back on her green leather seat.

"I know there was a load of false gods being worshipped before the Goddess," Failure stated. "Cos the Kala had all of them worshippers strung up or 'fixed or burned in Greenwich Park with the resistance fighters. Pa took me there sometimes when I was little, to get a bit of pick pocketing done in the crowds."

"I see," Atsiler nodded. "Failure, I would advise you not to mention anything outright illegal in your past from heretofore. If that's possible."

"Oh, the Guzzers just give you a slap on the neck for pickpocketing," Failure explained, helping herself to a handful of almonds. "So, it's not really an illegal thing, not really."

"I assure you," Atsiler replied. "That it is."

"Well, I'll pray for forgiveness then, m'love," Failure grinned. "Goddess be merciful."

Major Atsiler rose from her chair gracefully and walked across the grand lounge, the hum and creak of the yacht accompanying her. "The Kala was present at the Great Quake itself, Failure. In an area of the arctic known as Hadrovane. She was one of only five souls to be spared. Before the Kala made her escape, the Goddess rose from the icy waters before her. She gave instructions. The Kala must become the hope of the people. She must Reform and save the nation of Britain. She must weed out the false gods and the false sciences. She must champion the creation of travel through time, prevent the flooding of the natural world, before all life on earth is made extinct and—"

"Humans," Failure cut in.

Major Atsiler paused, disturbed from her flow. "What was that?"

"Before humans are made extinct. Not fish," Failure clarified. "Sharks, corals, the other things down there and stuff that came after the Quake; the Sylkies, and what not. They'll probably be ok."

The Major looked flustered. "I – well, that isn't the point." She shook her lustrous hair back from her shoulders. "The point is that the Kala and her Time Corp created the Time Programmes, to do the Goddess' bidding. Each year we begin a recruitment process to find the very best, most promising, most astounding young people we can. It is a great honour to have your education provided by the Time Corp, Failure. Most of the recruits that make it have been highly educated, trained, nourished and disciplined, drilled. In fact, most have been groomed to compete in the selection process their entire lives. It is a very great honour." There was a pause, as Atsiler eyed Failure. "Do you have any questions you would like to ask me?"

"Yeah, ok," Failure replied. "What happened to your eye?"

The Major smiled. "I know you better than you want me to, Failure," Atsiler said in a voice that was rich with the colours and scents of places Failure had never seen.

"You don't know me at all," Failure corrected.

"Oh, I do. Where do you suppose I grew up, kiddy?"

Failure stared, disarmed. "Where, m'lovely?" she asked tentatively.

"Never you mind. You can never escape where you're from, Failure. You can run from it. You can bury it. You can even make it work to your advantage, if you're smart. But I will always know who you really are. You keep your secrets for now," she said, "but if you want to get ahead, if you want to even stand a chance, you're going to have to start telling the truth. And you're going to have to start trusting people. You're going to have to want it more than anything else in this world. And you're going to have to learn to obey rules and to respect authority. In fact, on reflection, I don't think it would be wise to enter you into the selection process after all."

Unexpectedly, Failure's guts fell crashing to her knees.

"You have no sports or physical training," Atsiler went on. "No orienteering skills, accomplishments, general knowledge. No formal education of any kind, let alone expertise in engineering, extraordinary physical prowess or advanced knowledge of quantum mechanics. You would fail in every single test I can think to subject you to."

"I'm good at stuff when I put my mind to it," Failure interrupted, "and I'd have an advantage over every other kid you can put in for this selection thing. An advantage that would put me right at the front, when it came to going back. Travelling back in time, I mean."

"And what is that?" Atsiler asked.

"There's not a soul on this earth I give a goddam about leaving behind," Failure replied.

"You would fail the selection," the Major reasserted, her manner cool and blunt. "It is a certainty. And I don't want to waste anyone's time, especially not my own. So no, I will not be including you in the selection process. Instead, we will wait for these mists to clear and head North immediately."

"What d'you mean?" Failure asked.

"You would fail the selection, and so we will simply skip it. I'm going to take you straight to the Royal Scottish Time Programme. To begin work as a student."

CHAPTER NINE

Smith entered with the young man from the night before, who's handsome face was ugly with disdain. He wore a white t-shirt and jeans, and Failure now saw that the bare skin of his arms and neck were covered with all manner of tattoos; the Goddess, a mathematical code, a flaming torch, a compass. The ugly white bird who had torn the rabbit apart on the deck the night before was perched on his right shoulder, blinking.

"Good morning, Desi," Major Atsiler smiled. "I hope you had a comfortable night?"

"Blissful." He glared at her with no hint of good humour.

"I'll take that as a teenager's yes," Atsiler went on. "I wanted you to come and meet Failure. Failure, this is Despair. He's already a student at the Time Programme. A very gifted one, at that. He's been spending a little time in London Under reevaluating his priorities. But now, we head north once again."

"How north?" Failure asked, again the pang of homesickness threatening.

"The Royal Scottish Programme stands on an island off the north coast of Scotland," Atsiler replied. "Called Eylan Morr." A shadow passed over the Major's expression. "We have a long journey to make. The two of you will use the time to catch up on schoolwork. I've work to do. Don't cause any trouble. Any questions?"

"How'd you do your eye in?" Failure asked.

The Major stopped and turned back. "This is your last warning," she said quietly. "Learn to keep your mouth shut, or you'll be back here before you can say "failure"."

Leaving the boy and his bird scowling at the table, Failure pulled on her yellow Mac and headed out through the glass doors onto the sun deck. The boat beneath her feet lay unnaturally still, held in the cradling arms of the retreating silver mist. Failure stood by the cool metal rail and looked out into the eternal darkness of the sad, sinking city before her. The morning was hot and dark. Whale oil lamps flickered in their glass cases from the bank. The smog-blackened sky hung motionless above. The tops of the skyscrapers watched from the distance, slowly eaten alive by the flood. The boats bobbed on the brown river water, hiding the horrors below, and the sun-starved people went about their day on the water and the mud flats and the marketplaces, as though nothing had changed. Failure had never realised how beautiful it was, until now that she was destined to leave it.

With a creak, the glass doors opened and the boy followed Failure out onto the deck. He held his arm out wide and the white bird hopped down onto his forearm, then stretched her long wingspan, pushed off and soared up into the darkness. He watched her until she vanished, then caught Failure staring at him.

"There's a feast on Tower Bridge she could tuck into," Failure said. "If you don't mind your bird being fed on weeks' old rotten convict skin, that is."

"The more rancid the better," he replied. "She hates fresh meat."

"Is she a vulture, then? I only ever saw brown vultures before."

"Egyptian vulture. She's not from round here," he replied.

"Yeah, I guessed you were foreigners from the kiss on your skin," Failure told him. "And you're gifted, apparently. Do they watch all the gifted kids with an armed guard at this Time Programme place?"

The boy glanced across at the officers who had followed him onto the far side of the deck. "I'm reevaluating my priorities," the boy smirked. "Why're you here?"

"I'm joining as a student," Failure replied.

The boy frowned. "You mean you're going in for the selection process?"

"No, I'm skipping that whole thing, apparently," she shrugged.

"Well, that's gonna make you popular with the kids at the Programme," he said, no hint of humour in his level gaze. He stared at her with something searching in his cold brown eyes. The weight of his stare was unlike anything else Failure had known, as though he was trying to decipher her like a complicated map.

"I have a question for you," he said. "Why're your lips green? Is it a London Under thing?"

Failure covered her mouth with her fingers self-consciously. "I had the water blight, when I was younger. It can stain your lips, if you survive. It's faded a lot, though, and it'll probably go completely when I'm older. That's the only side effect I had," she lied, a little too aggressively. To change the subject, she asked, "How many are there? Time Programmes, I mean."

"One in each of the Kala's Principalities," he replied. "Scotland, England, Wales and Kernow. Remote. High ground. Heavily fortified against stuff like the weather and attack; surrounded by land or water mines, no-fly zones, guarded 24 hours a day."

"They sound more like prisons than schools," Failure mused.

"Yeah," he scowled. "As a matter of fact, Bodmin Programme in Kernow actually is an old prison. But Royal Scots is something else. Modern, purpose-built. It's in the guardianship of Baron LeoSirus."

"Never heard of him," Failure said, receiving a look of disbelief and dislike from the boy.

"He's the Kala's second eldest," Despair explained. "He lives on the north coast of the mainland. Edinburgh Castle."

"I guess it pays to be a Baron these days," Failure thought out loud. "I dunno if I like the sound of all this so much."

"Well, you'll be escaping this hell hole, so every cloud has a silver lining," the boy shrugged. "Except the ones here." He knelt down in the mist.

"You better not touch the mist," Failure warned. But the boy had already dragged his hand through the silver clouds. He held his hand up before himself and examined the soft, vanishing nothingness of the glowing silver that now clung to his fingers. He went to touch it to his lips and Failure leapt forward, grabbing his arm and wrenching his fingers away from his mouth.

"What're you thinking?" she cried. "Can't you see the mist's been trying to get a fix on us, trying to claim the goddam ship? Don't make yourself a target, or you're making us all targets."

"I heard London Undeners are a superstitious bunch," he smirked. "Too much salt and smog. And mist, apparently." He walked inside, leaving her alone on the deck.

There's something not right about that boy, warned her guts as they watched him closing the glass doors behind himself. *You should stay away from him.*

I don't think that's going to be possible, the pocket watch tripped.

Beneath her feet, the engines of the yacht kicked into being. Failure gripped the cold rail, as she was carried away from home for the first time in her life.

CHAPTER TEN

Around mid-morning the engines gave a subtle shift, and the yacht began to slow. At the same time, the guard shift changed and as Smith replaced one of the guards on the sun deck, Failure wandered outside once again. The silver mist was gone, as though it had never been there at all. And the eternal ceiling of black smog in the sky above was thinning rapidly. To the West, the land mass of Britain cast a murky shadow on the horizon. To the East, there was only the glittering sea, stretching out forever under the winter sun.

"Does it get a lot brighter than this?" Failure asked Smith, indicating the sky.

"A lot," Smith replied with a smile. "This is like dusk, in other places. Scotland included. One day you'll look back and wonder how you lived for so long in the dark."

"It's just normal to me," Failure replied. "This ne'er-do-well brightness is what's strange. Why're we slowing down?"

"That built-up area over there is the docks of Norwich-on-Sea," Smith told her, pointing to the land mass to the West. "We need to refuel. Won't take long."

Failure's eye was caught by a flicker of movement, far back on the distant horizon. She felt the unmistakable, though impossible, sensation of eyes upon her.

"...a deeply religious community, the people of Norwich-on-sea," Smith was saying. "And in fact, a lot of the religious texts you'll study at the Programme are being produced there these days, not least because they're so close to the papyrus paddies of South Lincolnshire..."

"There's another ship back there," Failure interrupted him. Smith glanced out over the empty horizon and shook his head.

He looked directly at her. "You don't need to be afraid anymore, Failure. You're very safe here, guarded and protected by the Kala's own people."

"But I feel like I saw something," she insisted.

"It's only natural if it takes you a while to adjust," Smith replied. But Failure stayed out on the deck as they approached the docks, occasionally scanning the horizon, though she saw nothing else.

Norwich-on-Sea was a small but busy dockland. Fishermen and ballast heavers went about their loading and unloading much the same as they did in London Under, but none of them were clothed in long Macs and sou'westers, none of them hobbling on blackened feet. Horses dragged carts along busy grey slabbed streets, leading to bustling marketplaces, cafes and temples. Red robed priestesses traversed the streets like blood in a vein, and dotted amidst it all were small stone roadside shrines, overflowing with flowers and painted pottery ornaments of the Goddess. Almost nobody wore a weapon, either strapped to their back or in their hand.

This is a different world, Failure's guts warned her.

Maybe this is what all other cities are like, the pocket watch ticked. *What if London Under's the oddity?*

Let's go and have a better look, Failure determined, adding aloud to Smith, "I'm going for a look about."

"Nice try," Smith smiled back, "but we're under orders that you stay on board."

"Oh, it's ok, I just want to go and have a look at the docks," Failure insisted. "I'm not going off round the city."

"Again, we're under orders to ensure you stay safely on board," Smith repeated.

"I'm not a prisoner here, you know," Failure told him. "I'm like… important now, or something. Ask the Major."

"The Major's the one who wants you to stay on board," he replied. "So, you stay on board."

With a fizzing crack, a fierce, magenta-pink light exploded

in the sky above the yacht, lighting up the dusky morning like a firework. A flare had been fired above them. The beautiful fizzing pink spray shone like a fountain. But the next moment, the boat lurched sickeningly to the starboard side. Failure was thrown sidewards, slamming face down onto the white deck. Her head sang with a shrill note as she blinked the pain away and started to right herself.

A heavy body slammed down on top of her, pinning her to the deck. She screamed in protest and tried to break free, as a dozen rapid thwacks split the air. She knew that sound. Knew what was coming the very next instant, even as the vicious volley of crossbow bolts slammed into the wall of the sun deck like a drumroll.

Smith's voice called urgently from where he had Failure pinned under his bear-like form, "Stay down and still. We're under attack."

CHAPTER ELEVEN

A rusty grappling hook sailed above Failure and Smith's heads. With a sickening thud, it bit its teeth around the railings of the sun deck. A hail of crossbow bolts rained down on the prow. Two boats were pulling up alongside the yacht, both crudely fortified with corrugated iron, wooden pikes and huge static whaling harpoons. The occupants were hanging off the defensive battlements and howling gleefully, scarves wrapped around their faces.

Bent low, but moving at pace, half a dozen guards filed out onto the yacht's deck, raising their harps in formation to return fire. In their midst, a Sergeant with close-cropped grey hair was un-casing a large, brown ball. With steady hands, she lit a long cream-coloured wick, which fizzed down towards the bomb and its deadly shrapnel secreted away inside. The flame raced lower, as a guard close-by was speared by the full force of a crossbow bolt. He slammed back on the deck, struggling like a beetle on its back, blood seeping from beneath his uniform.

"He'll bleed out," Failure called to Smith, trying to push his weight from her back as the Sergeant flung the firebomb. "You need to help him."

"Stay down," Smith barked at her. "You don't understand how important you—" Smith's voice was ripped from the air by a deafening *va-boom,* as the nearest of the two attacking boats exploded in a mess of plastic, metal, limbs, screams, iron and oil. The debris rained down on Smith and Failure with a splatter. Failure tried again to push Smith off her, and this time his limp body simply rolled away and onto the deck. A jagged chunk of twisted metal shrapnel was lodged into his back. A trail of blood seeped onto the white deck.

"Smith!" Failure called. "Come on, get up!" But as she tried to wake him, a pair of enormous, soaking-wet arms closed around her and lifted her clean from her feet. Failure kicked and writhed, but the grip around her chest was immense and her energy sapped away in moments.

"The weapons all go down!" came a deafening shout from above Failure's right ear. The voice was deep and thickly accented. The remaining officers spun around to face the source of the shout; their weapons raised to attack. But as they caught sight of Failure hanging in the clutches of the stranger, every officer lowered their harp or bow.

"There is another kid, yes?" called the pirate. "Where? You bring him here now, or I kill this one."

The doors to the sun deck opened with a sigh and Desi stepped out onto the deck. The look on his face was murder. His vulture swooped out after him on the hot air and settled on his shoulder. The kidnapper chuckled. He dropped Failure to the deck where at last she could get a good look at him.

He was as tall and broad as Smith, but older, with sun damaged skin, a long blonde beard and hair, tied up in a knot on his head. A thick scar twisted across one cheek and eye, distorting the corner of his mouth upwards like a permanent, lopsided smile.

"Good. We three. We go."

The second of the fortified boats pulled alongside the yacht and a rope ladder was thrown up to the kidnapper. Desi was the first to be sent down, where greedy, seeking hands grabbed at him. They were a filthy bunch, with beads and thread woven in their long hair, wearing necklaces of bone, ear and claw. Failure was pushed onto the bench beside Desi. The boy looked sideways and gave her a fierce, burning stare, then a little nod. She had no idea what it meant, but she nodded back all the same.

The boat's motor choked into life and they sped away from the yacht and the docks and Atsiler's protection. The crew whooped and jeered as they made their escape along the coastline, laughing and celebrating their catch. A woman with a shaved head tugged Failure's arms behind her back and tied her wrists with a line of aged, scratchy rope. A silver-haired man with no teeth in his gums was similarly tying Desi's hands. The large white bird soared above them, her bright wings and yellow feathers gleaming in the murky light. The kidnapper eyed the bird with a narrowing gaze.

"Why doesn't she fly away?" Failure muttered to Desi quietly.

He shrugged and said, "Stupid bird."

The boat veered gradually towards the shore and the kidnapper knelt before his catch. He regarded them one after the other, saying in a deep voice, "You be good. You stay quiet. No trouble, yes? We sell you. We sell you damage, we get bad money, understand? We sell you body good, brain good, we get good money. We sell you dead, we get no money. You good, no trouble for you. Ok? Now you tell this bird to be gone." He pointed at the white shadow above.

"It's not up to me," Desi said. "She's a vulture; not a puppy. She'll go where she likes."

With a fierce crack, the kidnapper slapped the boy hard across the face. The force sent Desi slamming to the deck, cracking his skull against the bench with a resounding *thunk*. The toothless old man dragged him back to a seated position and lifted Desi's chin towards the kidnapper, who repeated, "The bird. Tell it to be gone."

Desi spat blood to the deck. "Tell her yourself."

The kidnapper slung a second attack on the same painful, bloody spot as he had delivered the first. Desi was ready this time and braced himself with his feet against the deck, gritting his teeth and screwing his eyes against the pain. The kidnapper gestured to the woman with the shaved head, shouting something angrily in his native tongue. She threw him a crossbow.

That's an early version of the Zeeva model, Failure's guts rattled off automatically as she eyed the weapon. *Single trigger original, crudely re-rigged to have a four-trigger system. Looks good but has poor aim and no real power behind it.*

The kidnapper raised the crossbow, following the flight of the white bird. Failure felt Desi's body tense alongside her. "Fly on, Kezia," he called up into the hot winds above.

He's unlikely to hit his target unless it's in close range, Failure told her guts. *Trigger system's weakened by being messed with.*

That wasn't my point and you know it, her guts admonished. *That crossbow looks like one of Pa's. This gang were sent after you all the way from London Under. By him.*

With a thwacking sound, the kidnapper fired three bolts at the determined vulture. The bolts zinged towards her and Kezia soared out of their path like a kite on a current.

"Go on, fly on," Desi shouted up at the bird more aggressively now. Kezia circled higher, crying out, 'Ga-ga-ga-ga-ga-ga-ga-ga.' And then she changed course, soaring away from the boat and back toward the city. The kidnapper smiled broadly, as though he were the most handsome devil in the fifteen seas, then fired off a final, careless bolt.

The shot pinged with a high crack, and a terrible moment later the bird fell like a stone. Failure felt the boy's body go rigid with grief, as they both imagined the thud of the vulture's carcass landing on a distant street, becoming a feast for the first scavenger on the scene.

The boat drew up at a collapsing jetty outside an abandoned motorcar garage. It was scrawled with fading graffiti and peeling and rotting Time Corp posters; no one had been this way in a long time. From within, a wide metal door was hauled up before them, revealing the flooded interior of a garage. A young man emerged, dragging the boat inside, looking furtively out to the horizon. He had long, vivid ginger hair and two acid-green serpents tattooed across each of his cheeks.

"Where's the other boat?" he asked, his accent different to the others. "The number two boat?"

"We bring back the kids," the kidnapper cried, and the gang cheered and whistled, beginning to clamber out of the boat. "Now we make our money."

"But where's the other boat?" The young man demanded with a tremor in his voice. "Where is Annika?"

"Annika went out with blood screams on her lips and fight hard," the kidnapper cried back. "Now you get the goods. Be happy."

Amidst the hubbub and bustle of the disembarkation, Failure watched the red-haired young man from a corner of her eye. His skin had drained to a sickly green colour, and he muttered and grimaced as he slammed the heavy metal door back into place, plunging them into a deeper darkness. Failure caught Desi's eye and they shared a silent look, like two little rabbits having spotted the pie they were about to be baked into.

CHAPTER TWELVE

Failure and Desi were dragged through the garage and its litter of half-mended cars from ages past, their metal guts spilled and abandoned back in a time when fuel had become gold dust. The corridor beyond led to a steep set of stairs, and a cellar further in.

"Go down there," the woman with the shaved head commanded. Failure stepped carefully; her hands tied behind her back. Desi arrived beside her just moments before the heavy door at the top of the steps was slammed shut, and then locked. Complete, endless darkness engulfed them. The air smelled like the pavements after a storm; salty and earthy and stagnant all at once. Dripping water sounded from within the walls.

At least you aren't scared of the dark, the pocket watch ticked at Failure's chest, unusually loud in the darkness.

"Are you ok?" She whispered aloud to Desi.

"Yeah. You?"

"I'm ready to kick some goddam heads in."

"That's ideal," Desi replied. "But first we need to get out of this cellar. Otherwise, Atsiler doesn't stand a chance at tracking us. Have you got any weapons hidden on you? A knife or something?"

"No," Failure replied, "but we don't need a knife for the ropes. The girl who did my wrists tied a sawline, I think. You?"

"No idea," he breathed back. "I don't know anything about knots."

"Well, I do," Failure grinned, "and this rope's cheap and old. Big sudden moves should do it. Hang on…" With several violent jerks, the bonds of the sawline eased enough for Failure to reach her fingers upwards and pull the knot apart.

"I'm out," Failure grinned again. "Where are you?" Fingers tingling and wrists throbbing, she reached out in the darkness for the boy in the void.

"I'm here," he told her, as her hands collided with his chest. Failure traced a line down one of his arms and found his wrists and the ropes which bound them.

"There, you're free," she said in a whisper as she eased the bonds and the rope fell away. Together, they clambered the steps and listened at the locked door. Hearing no one beyond, they pulled and pushed and fiddled with the lock. But there was no escape that way. They descended back into the dripping, stale salt-scented abyss and set about examining every inch of the cellar, feeling their way laboriously through the dark. But there was no chink in the wall. No way of tunnelling or climbing. Despondent, Failure sank to the damp brick floor and rested her back and head against the wall.

"Ok," Desi's voice came from the other side of the cellar. "What else have you got up your sleeve?"

"What d'you mean?" Failure asked.

"Well, I happen to have overheard some pretty intense stuff about you last night – bombs and time mirages and goddess knows what."

"I don't usually just carry bombs around," Failure sighed. "I just stole that one for a friend."

"Well, if you have some sort of other superpowers then this is the time to tell me. They said there was a time mirage in the park, and that you were right in the middle of it."

"I can't... I really don't remember it," Failure lied.

"The point is," came Desi's voice from the darkness, "It would be extremely helpful right now if you could just time travel us out of here."

"Well, you're out of luck, cos I can't," Failure sighed. "Is your face ok? That guy smacked you down pretty bad on the boat."

"I'm fine," he replied shortly, then added, "Can you hear a ticking sound?"

Failure's hand went to the pocket watch which hung at her chest. She heard him climb to his feet. "Sounds like a motor or something. It's faint but... there, can you hear it?"

"It's just my watch," Failure replied, feeling the renewed weight of the solid gold contraband. "I've got an old-fashioned pocket watch, one you have to wind up. Nothing we could use. Actually, it's on a chain, so we could use the chain to sort of garrotte someone. If we could get close enough."

"I see," came the despondent response, and the sound of the boy sitting back down against a wall.

"So, you're a runaway?" she asked the darkness.

"Let's call me an escapee," his voice replied. "I climbed into the dirty laundry bins and got wheeled aboard the monthly supply boat. When we got to Waverly Docks in Edinburgh I snuck out and bribed a trader to take me all the way to London Under. I was told it was a good place to disappear. But they found me, of course. Apparently, I stuck out like a sore thumb."

"Bad luck," Failure offered.

"I was brought to Atsiler a couple hours before you were," Desi went on. "To be escorted back to Eylan Morr and The Royal Scottish Time Programme. Meanwhile the authorities have been to my home and rounded up my entire family. They said they were going to escort them to Hullondon."

"The capital?"

"Yep, to one of the Biodomes," he replied darkly. "A special favour to the family of a star Time Programme student. Clean air and security from the weather. Everything they could ever need. It's a dream come true."

"But they're actually hostages?" Failure finished for him. "To guarantee that you don't run away again."

"You said it, not me," Desi sighed.

"Why did you run away in the first place?" Failure asked.

"Because of Eylan Morr," Desi replied, with a cold bleakness in his voice. "The island. They should never have built a school on that place. Or anything. People have been trying to build or settle or work there for thousands of years. Over and over again. But every time humans have tried to harness that island, they've ended up evacuating it in misery. Bad things happen on Eylan Morr. Lighthouse keepers going missing three at a time, with no sign of struggle. Shepherds losing whole flocks of sheep over the cliffs. Whole villages losing their minds."

"So, you ran away cos you were scared?" Failure asked.

"Escaped," Desi corrected again. "And it wasn't just the island… It's a big honour to get into the Programme, especially amongst the kids of the Barons. We're under a lot of pressure."

"Are you…" Failure faltered for a moment, "are you the kid of a Baron?"

"Yeah," Desi replied, and then, in the dark void, he laughed out loud.

"Why're you laughing?" Failure asked, embarrassed.

"It's just sort of funny," Desi replied. "Most people would just be able to tell. But you're so… it's like you're brand new. No idea about stuff."

"I think I'm kind of goddam old," Failure smiled into the darkness. "Anyway, if it's this big honour, then didn't you want to stay?"

"At first, yeah," he mused. "But then you really, really start thinking about it. The technology is a one-way ticket. It can only send you back. No return journey. That only seems real when you're suddenly looking it in the face. You aren't meant to care. It's for the good of mankind. It's the only way to save us all. We have to get back and stop the Great Quake. That's all that matters. But if you've got anything here in this world that you love, then it suddenly looks like a death sentence."

"So, your family are decent, are they?" She asked.

"Yeah," Desi said, an aching in his voice. "They really are. I grew up landlocked in the Black Country. The floods didn't feel so… you know."

"Like you're being eaten alive?" Failure offered.

"Like you're being eaten alive," Desi echoed. The darkness weighed upon them. "I loved home," he said, more quietly. "Fields, woods. A few small market towns and a few canals for traders. Most people just farmed and paid their taxes; went to worship the Goddess on Saturdays; enjoyed the Pagan festivals when they rolled around year after year after same-old year; got married to someone sweet from the next village; laboured hard, had kids, died with their family all around them. I had a lot of friends, back home. And we kept birds of prey." As he said the last three words, the bloody, white ghost of the vulture Kezia swooped down to haunt their midnight prison.

"For hunting?" Failure asked, trying to dispel the ghost. "Or fighting?"

"What d'you mean, fighting?" Desi asked.

"You know, fights," Failure replied. "Cock fights. Dog fights. Man against pack, all that stuff."

"That's just the weird sort of thing you'd say," he said, the shine of laughter again in his words. "Our birds were just show birds. People liked to watch them fly."

"Oh, right," Failure said, but she had never heard of such a thing.

"Kezia was always strange," he went on, keeping his voice low. "They don't recognise their masters, birds of prey. We raise them from the cradle to the grave and still they'd never know us from the next meat-holding-glove. But she always knew me. Stupid bird."

"She was kind of gross, anyway," Failure said. "Next time you get a pet you could have yourself a nice little ferret or a kitten. Even a rat would be an upgrade. Or else make it really easy on yourself; get a fish, set it free."

Desi made a sound in the darkness. Failure did not know him well enough to distinguish whether it had been a laugh or a sob, or both.

"Maybe she wasn't hit," Failure said into the nothingness. "He might have missed her. She might have just dived down to avoid the bolt and flown off."

"Yeah," Desi sighed. And after a long pause he added, "Thanks for saying it."

And then, from above, the silence was broken by a quiet rattle of chains, a jangling of keys, and the slow, barely audible creak of the door opening.

CHAPTER THIRTEEN

The warm flicker of a firefly lamp spread into the cellar. Holding the lamp at the top of the stairs was the ginger-haired youth with acid-green snake tattoos on his cheeks. He held a spiked club. Three shadowed figures huddled behind him. He spoke in an urgent whisper. "You want live, you come with me."

Without a second thought, Failure bolted for the stairs and raced to the summit. Desi followed. The ginger youth led them stealthily through the abandoned garage and came to a halt at a red fire exit, which led to the outside world. He paused and glanced back at his followers. After taking a deep breath, he turned to the door, raised a leg high and kicked the door hard with his boot. It burst open and they fled into the open air.

Whether these mutineers had taken pity on them, or intended to ransom them off themselves, Failure had no idea. But either way she pelted in the midst of them down a long cobbled street. As they turned a corner ahead, the fire door banged open again, amidst yells. The other gang members were already in pursuit. The familiar thwack of a crossbow bolt rent the air, and the woman beside Failure fell like a sack of blubber to the paving. Another pained scream sounded as a young blonde kid also went down, a crossbow bolt sticking from his calf. He reached after his two vanishing friends and screamed imploringly, but their pace never slowed.

They ran and emerged onto a wide city road. The tarmac was densely carpeted with a crop of superweed, and a Time Corp billboard showed a tall, elegant girl, with long braided hair, standing proud, holding a forefinger out to the Kala. Her other hand was raised in a military salute. Her muscular figure was apparent through her grey t-shirt and black shorts, her skin a blaze of colour with Triumph badge tattoos. "Penitence McCleod! The Kala salutes you! Go bravely in the past!"

Just short of the billboard, the ginger youth skidded to a halt, shouting something to his one remaining companion, the woman with the shaved head. They both turned to face the oncoming pursuers. It was time to fight or die. Perhaps both. The youth knelt to touch the earth, then stood tall and raised the spiked club in his hands. The woman with the shaved head drew out a meat cleaver and licked her lips.

"Throw me a weapon," Failure shouted to the ginger-haired youth. "You're outnumbered, we're gonna be slaughtered. Let me fight!"

With a pained desperation, the ginger youth ripped a bag from his back and threw it to her. Failure caught the bag and raced to the billboard wall nearby, fumbling with the cord ties. The pursuers closed in.

"Failure. Come this way." Desi's voice. It came, impossibly, from behind the Time Corp billboard which hung limply from its brackets at Failure's side. It stirred in a warm current of wind and Failure saw a concealed alleyway. She slipped behind it and was gone.

The alleyway was narrow and dark and still. Desi stood four paces ahead of her. Before him, the paving slabs sloped directly into brown, stagnant water. Norwich-on-sea was going under. A host of naked plastic mannequins lay perfectly still on the surface, face down or staring blankly up at the sky, like the victims of a horrific crime. The water they lay in was too still, too dense and too dark to be the water of the old world.

"We'll have to go through it," Desi whispered, staring at the mannequin-strewn pool ahead.

"We can't," Failure hissed back. "This place is going under, just like home. Look at the water. It's not... It might not be safe. We'd be better trying to get up on the roofs and running for it."

"That's exactly what they'll assume we'll do," Desi whispered, gesturing back to the main road, where the sounds of an almighty brawl had broken out. "Whoever wins that fight will be up on the rooftops in a matter of minutes."

"If this place is anything like home, then the water's worse than the kidnappers," Failure hissed, automatically touching her green-stained lips. Desi's eyes followed her fingertips and lingered there.

"I know it's dangerous," he whispered. "But they will find us on the roofs. I'm going into the water."

"Good luck, then," Failure told him, pulling the ginger youth's backpack onto her back. "Gives us both better odds, anyway if we're apart." They glared at one another, as the grunts, screams and clashing metallic crunches of the fight sounded beyond. Desi's stare seemed to pass through Failure's eyes and skin, beyond her ribs and directly at her armoured heart, which thudded its warning of danger.

"I can see that you're clever, and brave," Desi whispered. "You're kind of weird too. And you're from a tough place. I bet you've never really trusted anyone in your life, but you're going to have to trust me now. They will look on the rooftops first. They will find you. However bad the water might be, it's your only chance."

Desi reached out and took one of Failure's hands in his. His skin was warm and she could feel the bones beneath.

Get on that rooftop and run for it, cried Failure's guts. *Let go of his hand right now and let him cause a distraction by getting eaten alive by Sylkies.*

"In the water I'm in charge," Failure told Desi. "You do what I say."

"Always," he replied. For the very first time, his face broke out in a grin. One deep, sharp dimple appeared in each of his cheeks.

Don't touch his face, you idiot, Failure's guts commanded. *You're going to have to use every one of your very few brain cells to concentrate on navigating the deadly water.*

Why would I touch his goddam face? Failure fumed back, but her guts had given up on her.

Hand in hand, Failure and Desi waded into the icy water. It was still as death, murky and brown as mussel chowder. Together they stepped deeper, pushing the plastic mannequins away like rubber ducks at a fair. The sticking, biting cold claimed their bodies inch by inch until they were chest deep. When they reached the brick wall at the far end, Failure sank down to her neck, skimming the lichen covered bricks with her hands.

"Wall's too slippy to climb," she said, "But there must be some gap letting the flood through. I'll find it. Better hope it's big enough to squeeze through." So saying, she took a deep breath, sealed her lips and ducked beneath the surface. At last, her hands met with a large hole close to the cobbles. When she resurfaced and scrubbed her face and eyes clear, the sounds in the street beyond had changed. Now someone was hitting something repeatedly, with grunts of effort. There were no return blows.

"Time to go," Failure hissed. "Take a really deep breath and don't swallow any goddam water."

CHAPTER FOURTEEN

The narrow street beyond was lined with ancient buildings, whose slanted walls and black wooden beams leaned in towards one another at impossible angles.

"We should rise out of this lagoon up ahead and then we can run for it," Failure hissed, keeping her head above the water and swimming steadily. "If this place is going under then it's all about finding a boat, now."

"Is that the lore of a city that's going Under?" Desi asked alongside her.

"Yeah, that," Failure glared back at him, "and stay out of the water."

"Why is it so dangerous?" Desi asked, breathless in the cold.

"Salt-bite," Failure replied. "It's like an infection. All the tidal workers get it. It's like each time you're in the water it nibbles away at you. Over time, the water rots through the skin and the bone and everything. First, it goes black, then stuff just falls off. Doesn't kill you, just feeds off you. And then there's the Blight."

"What's blight?" Desi's lips were turning slightly blue, as though in sympathy for her own.

"It came one summer and never left," Failure replied. "There was this girl staying at The Townhouse. She shouldered the Loss. Her mum and dad bred poisonous snakes."

"Of course they did," Desi sighed with a roll of his brown eyes.

"The kids I knew growing up were the most cutthroat, nasty, backstabbing bunch of neverspeaks you could imagine," Failure told him. "But Loss was different. She told me about stuff she'd seen on her travels. Forests creeping into forgotten towns. White cliffs crumbling into the sea. Endless cracked concrete motorways, stretching in all directions, 'like the shattered bones of the country,' she said. That was how she talked. I thought she was like a bird, who'd seen the whole world." Failured paused for a moment while a warm smile crept onto her face.

"That summer we swam down into this old Museum, full of dinosaur bones. When we got back that afternoon, we both started feeling hot and weird and shivery. I don't remember anything else. Pa and Winston paid McGuvvorn to look after me for days. Plied me with moonshine for the pain, and seaweed to draw out the poison. When I came round, I was alive, and my lips were green as grass. But Loss wasn't so lucky. She was already starting to… you know." Failure glanced over at Desi through the icy lapping water between them.

"I don't know," he replied.

"Starting to change," Failure said, the cold seeping into her own bones, now.

"Change how?" He asked.

"Into one of them," Failure replied. "The eyes go first. Blacken. See shadows. So, the worst had to be done. You can't let someone change; for their sake and your own. More and more people got the sickness after that summer. More and more lights started shining under the surface of the water. And there wasn't no more swimming after—" Failure's boot bumped against something hard in the water and she faltered.

"Looks like it's getting shallow up ahead," Desi was gesturing to a steep cobbled street a few metres away. But Failure had frozen. Beneath her, there was a shadow. Large and dark and still. Ahead was another, similar in size and shape, equally still. And more behind. Something was floating, down beneath them.

You're swimming above some kind of herd, her guts warned frantically, her heart thudding like the hooves of a racehorse.

"There's something beneath us—" Failure whispered, but the words were snatched from her lips, as, with an agonising wrench, something grabbed hold of her ankle. It twisted and tugged, and with a scream of bubbles, Failure was dragged downwards.

Rainbow daggers of agony burned through the ankle which the creature held. The pain was worse than the electricity fired into her neck by Pa's eel. But poor dead Harry Fulcher had shown Failure how to get out of scrapes like this. In fact, he had formed a habit of grabbing her in the bar when she was the only one there, of grabbing her in the Townhouse's back corridors, of grabbing her in the darker streets of Fitzrovia. He would pin her against a wall or get her in a headlock; teaching her how to escape, so he said. Failure hadn't liked that game, so had learnt to escape pretty quickly. And it was now written in her bones, even in this moment, as something monstrous dragged her downwards through poisoned water.

Failure twisted herself at a series of bizarre angles and the attacker lost its hold. Lungs tearing, Failure kicked her good leg until she burst from the surface for a breath. But the monster was fast and grabbed for her ankle again. Without the luxury of surprise, it made a bad grip this time and Failure twisted free again, kicking away. But when the grip clamped her ankle for a third time, it locked like a vice.

Failure kicked. She twisted. But struggle and writhe and churn as she may, the grip held firm. She could not seem to break free. Poor dead Harry Fulcher had never grabbed her in the water, after all. Slowly, the creature pulled her beneath. Failure desperately tried to wrench herself away, back towards the surface, screaming bubbles rushing to their own escape. She saw her old friend Loss, swimming up above her, laughing and curling in the water, stolen treasure in her hands. She saw Winston baking bread in clouds of bubbles like steam. She saw Pa through the surface, laughing like a madman as she slingshotted bottles off a wall. And then she saw Desi, reaching out for her through all of the rest of them with his strong, painted arms. She grabbed for his shirt, his skin, his shoulders. And they really were there, not a mirage, but solid and real in the water.

Failure began a renewed campaign of viciously kicking at the grip that held her, as Desi dragged her upwards against the pull of the monster. With a final, violent kick, the grip on Failure's ankle loosened and was gone. She and Desi rose from the depths like corks popping from champagne bottles and dragged themselves to the shallows.

Failure crawled out of the lagoon on hands and knees, coughing and spluttering beside Desi. She felt for the snakeskin wallet, which was still mercifully tucked in her back pocket, and touched her hand to her chest to feel for her pocket watch. It was gone. A glint of bright gold caught her eye on the cobbles beyond the shallows, and she saw the pocket watch, lying there, its chain trailing in the water. Desi, drenched to the bone and climbing to his feet close by, bent to pick it up.

"That's mine," Failure called. But as she put weight on her damaged ankle it exploded in agony. Failure cried out as she fell back onto the cobbles, grabbing the ankle as though she could protect it from itself.

If you can't walk, her guts told her, *you can't get away. Not to escape in a boat. Not even to hide.*

Desi stood silhouetted against the end of the narrow passage ahead. A grim expression clouded his face, like smog moving over the sun. The watch hung down from his hand by its chain.

"I'm mincemeat," Failure said in a choked voice. "Goddam weak bones. Goddam London Under lack of goddam sun."

Desi said nothing.

"You know what we do to dogs when they break a leg?" Failure asked him. "We put them out their misery."

Desi continued to stare at her. "Is there anything useful in that backpack?" His voice had become blank. Businesslike. He knew what had to be done. He had to leave her behind.

Failure held the bag out to him. "I haven't even looked – but you should take it. Just give me my watch back before you go."

Desi pulled the backpack over his shoulders. He crouched

beside Failure and, as though awarding her a medal, gently looped the chain of the pocket watch over her head.

"Good luck," she said, into the narrow space between them. "I hope you make it. And thanks for dragging me out of there."

The water had stripped the boy of his surety and his swagger. The bleached core of him was something less formed. "Put your arms around my neck," he said quietly.

"Why?" Failure breathed.

"I'm going to carry you," was his reply.

A fool's errand, ticked the pocket watch.

Don't listen to that old ticker, cried her guts.

It'll make you both too slow, the watch ticked on.

Who cares! Get him to drag us by the broken ankle if needs be! her guts insisted. *Stay here alone and you're dead.*

You'll be too visible, too vulnerable, ticked the golden watch. *This way is death for you both.*

"You need to run for the docks," Failure told Desi. "Get a boat or get in amongst the crowds. Wait for Atsiler to track you down. You can come back for me later, when she's found you."

"You know you won't make it," Desi said.

"Yeah, well," she sighed. "One of us might as well get away."

Like the brightest ray of burning London Under sunshine spearing through the smog, a grin cracked across Desi's eyes and lips. The expression was so shocking and so out of place, in this most terrible of moments, that Failure almost punched him in the face.

"Why in the name of mother goddess are you smiling?" She demanded.

"Shut up and listen," he replied. "We're staying together. We're both getting out of here. I'm going to carry you somewhere safe, see if we can splint your ankle and find something you can use as a crutch. Once you can move more easily, we head for the river, find a hiding place and stay put. Now let's get the hell away from that water."

Failure put her arms around Desi's neck and interlaced her fingers. With one arm on her back and one beneath her knees, he lifted her into a cradle hold. Beneath the cold skin of her right forearm, Desi's heart beat rapidly, as though it was trying to tell the blood in her own veins some desperate message. His skin smelt of salt. Grit crystals from the poisoned water were forming across his lips and eyelashes. The water was trying to claim him, and to Failure, he suddenly felt like home. Leaving only one set of sodden footprints behind on the paving slabs, they began to move, far too slowly, down the narrow street.

CHAPTER FIFTEEN

The tannery had once been a hospital. A huge building of reddish-brown brick, surrounded by iron fencing, who's Eastern wing was going under. On the muddy lawns before them, dozens of skins hung on dozens of brackets, in various states of treatment; some fresh off the back of the unfortunate seals, some almost dried and coated enough to be sold. The scent of boiling fat and pulverised brain hung heavy in the air.

Failure and Desi were met at the main entrance by a haggard looking man who agreed to rent them a room for four thousand a night, which was everything Desi had.

"You injured then, hun?" The man asked Failure in a thick Norfolk accent.

"Nah, we just got married, hun," she replied with a wicked grin. "My true love's got to carry me over the threshold, hasn't it?"

"Bleeding kids," the man muttered, but took the handful of soggy cash. He showed them up several flights of dark concrete stairwells to the top floor and their room, which had once been a hospital ward.

Desi deposited Failure onto a chair, making her wince and grit her teeth as her swollen ankle bumped against the cold floor. The smell of the seal hides wafted in through cracks in the windowpanes and strange sounds drifted up from the rest of the unfamiliar building; voices calling, banging, singing and the bark of a dog.

"This is good," Failure said as the old man left them. "We can see for miles. Only two doors as well, that's not too tricky to manage. First things first is to check where that other door goes to. Desi?"

"Yeah, good idea," he said. But his voice was heavy and tired, as though he hadn't slept for a hundred years. He threw the backpack to Failure, saying, "I'll check it out. You see what's in that."

The bag held a canteen of a purple liquid, with the same translucent, pearly gleam as Pa's moonshine; a single sodden flare, which Failure stood out to dry; and a few pieces of squid jerky.

"It doesn't lead anywhere except out onto the roof," Desi explained as he returned, moving like Atlas with the world on his shoulders, wandering across to one of the beds and collapsing down on it. "There's no one else up there, so we're fine here for now."

Failure threw him a few chunks of squid jerky, tucking in to some herself.

"Any dry clothes in there?" He asked, on a heavy, rasping breath. "I'm so cold. I'm cold in my... I dunno, in my bones. Is it getting dark already? There's like... shadows."

A nasty doubt prickled the hairs on Failure's arms. She licked her lips nervously. They always talked about the shadows.

"Ok, well, shadows can't hurt you," she reassured him. "Hey, Desi, don't go to sleep. You need to get those wet clothes off. Wrap yourself up in one of those old sheets as a blanket."

"You just wanna see my Triumphs," he grinned, as he peeled off his grey Time Programme t-shirt. His skin was turning a deathly white, beaded every inch with pearls of sweat, his breathing shallow and fast. A rasp sounded with every breath he drew in, like the drag of a saw through bone.

Failure unscrewed the canteen of pearlescent purple liquid, unleashing a sharp waft of star anise. She took a small swig and grimaced at the bitter brew. "Here, have a drink of this," she called, passing the bottle across to him. Desi took a sip. The drink made him cough and most of the fluid ran back out across his cheek.

"I'm not doing well, am I?" He asked, eyes half closed where he lay. A pair of tears rolled down his cheeks, dark in colour with a rainbow sheen, like oil.

"You'll be ok," Failure told him. "I know what to do."

You need seaweed, her guts told her. *And you might need a sharp axe, if it comes to that.*

"What did you mean, in the lagoon earlier?" Desi asked on ragged breath. "About the girl you knew? You said she started changing. That the worst had to be done."

"Oh yeah, I meant she started changing as in getting worse," Failure lied. "And that the worst had to be done as in, we had to watch her die. But that's not gonna happen to you. She'd been deep diving in poisoned water for days on end. You just had a little monster-themed sheep dip and probably swallowed a couple of gulps."

Desi stared at the ceiling with eyes stricken by shadows. "You're lying to me."

"You're not going to die," Failure told him, a hot flush of red rising on her cheeks. "I just need to find seaweed. We've got not cash, so I've just got to get to the coast and harvest some."

"Get to the coast," Desi said feverishly. "Go fishing for seaweed. Climb back out the water. Make it all the way up here. Without being seen. All on an ankle you can't use. Doesn't sound like the best plan."

"Well, I'm all you've got," Failure replied. "I'll be back soon."

You could sell me, the pocket watch ticked at Failure from its chain. *I'm gold. There must be a black market in Norwich-on-Sea. If you have cash, you have anything.*

Failure pulled on the backpack and moved painstakingly across the room and out, dragging the swollen ankle along like a dead rat.

As she reached the corridor beyond, the nauseating pain overwhelmed her, making the world shimmer and slide from side to side. Failure stopped moving to regain focus, feeling a wash of heat and then ice pass over her as she hung her head low. If she continued like this, she would pass out. Desi was right. She couldn't make it down the ten flights of stairs, let alone all the way to the river and back.

Footsteps sounded on the staircase below. A woman appeared, attractive with wiry black hair, threadbare red dress and olive skin.

"Alright there hun," she said, pointing a forefinger skywards, sending her luck to the Kala. "You're new here, isn't it?"

"Just arrived with my newlywed husband, hun," Failure lied. "I shoulder the Failure."

"Nice to meet you, Failure. I'm too old for them to have sent my name to mother goddess, so I'm just plain old Lorna. You aren't a local, are you?"

"Kala keep you, Lorna. And no, I married a local man, but I'm from London Under, you see. How long's Norwich-on-sea been going under?"

"Last five years," Lorna replied. "It in't comin from the sea though, hun. Tha's like it's coming up from under the streets themselves."

"Same in London Under," Failure told her. "But worse along. You work in the water?"

"I was a mudlark on the Wensum," Lorna replied. "Got my own little gang of kids now, so I don't have to go down in the water these days, I send them in instead. How about you?"

"I was up at the blubber processing plant up in Battersea," Failure lied. "But I've done my leg in, so I came up to Norfolk to see what's doing. Found me a husband. But I need a bit of seaweed, and this leg is being a pain today. You got a cup going spare? I've got a nice snakeskin wallet here you might like?"

Lorna laughed and said, "I wouldn't get out of bed for some fancy junk like that. And my bed's full of lice."

"What about one of your larks, they could run out and get me some, if they fancied? They could flog the snakeskin and give you half the earnings? You don't have to lift a finger. All for a spot of seaweed."

Lorna cocked her head, considering. "If one of them wants the work, I'll send them up to you."

"That's a deal," Failure nodded, eagerly.

"We'll be back out on the river the day after tomorrow," Lorna went on. "No idea where they are between times, so it'll have to wait 'til then."

Without clean water and seaweed Desi wouldn't make it through another two nights.

"Well, nice to meet you, Failure," Lorna smiled a gappy grin. "Maybe I'll see you round the dive."

Failure gritted her teeth and called, "Hey, I've something else you might be interested in."

With a deep heaviness in her heart, Failure reached inside her yellow rain mac and drew out the long chain and furiously ticking watch. She let it spin there for a second, glinting in the gloom. Lorna stepped closer and peered at the watch with dark brown eyes. "An old pocket watch," she mused. "I guess they're still fashionable in London Under, are they? Well, in the East these days all that's got value is fresh food and holy water. Nice try though. You in't in some sort of trouble, are you?"

Failure shook her head, tucking the watch back inside her jumper. "No, just fancy a bit of seaweed for our supper. See you around."

The piercing heat of a December noon fell over the city as Failure dragged herself back to Desi's sick bed and gave him the last of the bitter aniseed liquor.

"We used to go camping, when we were kids," Desi told her with a rasp in his voice. "My sisters and me. Have you got any sisters?"

"No," Failure replied. "It's just me."

"What about your parents?" Desi asked.

"Well, I never knew my dad, and my mum died before I was a year old. She was murdered. It was a big secret when I was growing up," Failure sighed. "I was only a baby when it happened, but I was in the room. I shouldn't remember it, really. Kids don't have memories from that early normally, do they? But I guess it got stuck in my brain somehow cos I have nightmares about it all the time. No one was meant to speak about it," Failure went on. "About the murder, I mean. But there was this card shark, Winston. He used to go with Pa for a few years, on and off. Well, Pa got him to tell me all about it one night, when they'd smoked a whole posy of seagrass. It was my ninth winter solstice. Pa thought that was the first I ever heard about it; I think. And he forgot everything the next day. Winston made me swear not to ever mention it again."

"What happened to her?" Desi asked.

"Well, if what I've sort of pieced together is right, then she was up in her apartment, on the top floor of The Townhouse. That's the building I grew up in. You'd know it, if you'd grown up on the wrong side of London Under. In the evenings, they said, my mother liked to wear a silk kimono and put makeup on her face, sat in front of a big silver mirror, getting ready to go out dancing. She performed in the musical hall. Wearing fur and perfume.

"On this night she had sat little baby Failure in a tiny tin bathtub, filled with bubble bath and champagne. Real stuff. And I was splashing in the bubbles. She'd painted my face in makeup, like a little doll, but it was dripping off like the doll was melting. And she was laughing or crying or both, playing scratchy records on a wind-up gramophone and lighting more and more oil lamps and filling firefly jars, lighting the room up brighter and brighter like a spell. She knew they were coming. And she hadn't even locked the door. The killer came in and stabbed her. That was it."

The wind sighed through the broken windowpanes.

"I don't know what to say," Desi murmured.

"Well, like I said, I was just a baby at the time," Failure replied hastily. "I can't remember it much, so it's totally fine. I'm not upset about it or anything."

Desi stared back at her with his conker brown eyes, the horror hanging over them as thick as mist on the Thames Broad. He held out a hand, and she took it. After a while, he fell into a deep, restless sleep. Failure held the weight of his hand. She imagined the skeleton inside him, the veins and the ligaments, the muscles and the organs each in their place, the skin wrapping around him like a Winter Solstice gift. She turned his hand over in hers, uncovering the veins on the inside of his wrist. Between the lines of tattoo ink depicting a black and golden chalice, his blood was still flowing blue inside his sun browned skin.

I can't bear to watch him die, she told the watch silently.

It's worse than that and you know it, the pocket watch ticked and tripped against her chest. *If the sickness takes him, he might start to change. You're already checking his veins for signs of rusty red. If it happens, you know what you have to do.*

I don't have a weapon, Failure told the ticking of the watch.

The windowpanes are cracked, the watch told her. *You can get glass shards with no trouble. You'll have to do it with your bare hands.*

Failure pressed the pocket watch against her beating heart and held it there.

There isn't a single person who you wouldn't put out of their misery, her guts spoke up, bitterly. *Even our worst enemy. If they were going to change, you would free anyone from that.*

But she couldn't do it to this boy, the pocket watch thrummed. *She'd rather he changed and ripped her throat out.*

"I'm so sorry I couldn't save us," she said aloud. "But I can't even get out of the building, let alone to the river. Seaweed is the only cure. It draws out the poison. Returns the water to itself. It saved me, and I spat the colour of seaweed for months after, and I've never really got the taste out of my mouth…" The words died on her lips, as the answer came to Failure like a streak of sunlight through the smog clouds. She had survived. She had never got the sickness again. The answer was right there inside her. The taste that had never quite left her green-tinged lips. Failure licked her finger and painted saliva onto Desi's mouth, like a strange sort of lipstick. His skin was frighteningly hot to the touch.

"Are you there?" his voice came from inches beneath her.

"Yes, I'm here," she said. "I'm putting… well, I'm putting my spit on your lips. Sorry, I know it's rank, but I think maybe the seaweed medicine is in me, in my body, like living inside me, and you need it, and this is the fastest way."

With a flutter like the first beat of a butterfly's wings, he opened his eyes. They were almost entirely black, the conker brown a waning crescent behind his ever-widening pupils. Thick, black oily tears streamed down his cheeks.

"Failure," he breathed, and she moved closer to hear his words. "Just kiss me."

"Well, I could do, I suppose," she said, her heart hammering a warning in her throat. "I guess that would be a quicker way of getting all this spit into you."

"Failure," he said again hoarsely, a shadowed smile promised in his black eyes. "I think I'm going to die. And I just want to kiss you."

Her heart flickered. It wondered.

You are not to get involved in this! her guts cried to her heart, incandescent with rage. *Don't wake up now. You can't be trusted. I've kept her safe all this time.*

But Failure was already kissing him. Desi's lips tasted of star anise and sun-fed grass and the sharp sea salt of home. The barricades around Failure's heart began to crack. Vicious, jagged knives found the chinks and prised open the armour, forged of five hundred million moments of a life without love. The barricades fell away like lichen torn from brick, leaving raw red heart flesh thumping painfully in her chest.

With a rusty creak, the door to the room was pushed open and an urgent voice shattered the stillness. "Oi, hun, is someone looking for you?" Lorna, the black-haired woman in the dirty red dress stood on the threshold. "There's a bunch of neverspeaks just pushed their way inside, goin' room to room. Rough bunch, I don't like 'em. Looking for a girl and a lad that sounds bad like you."

"We're in big trouble, hun," Failure cried.

"They're guarding the ways in and out downstairs, so you got no hope that way," Lorna told her quickly. "I told them I never saw the likes up on this floor, but they'll come looking. We don't like no one throwing muscle round in this building, so I come to warn you."

"Please," Failure cried imploringly, reaching out to Lorna across the void of empty space. "Please, can you help me get him up on the roof? We might be able to hide out there."

"I've warned you they're coming," Lorna snapped. "That's good enough."

"Please!" Failure begged as Lorna turned to go. "I'll do anything!" Something in Failure's strangled plea made the woman pause and turn back. She sighed deeply, shaking her head. "I loved a boy once," she mused longingly. "I used to sing him shanties, from the docks. He said I was a songbird. I'd even sing to him in his sleep. He up and left me for a skirt in Caister-on-Sea, that summer before the Great Quake. They both drowned, far as I know. I didn't even shed a tear. But I loved him once, I did. I'll get you to the roof and then I'm gone."

CHAPTER SIXTEEN

The roof was sickeningly high, the wind whipping about them in long ribbons. The air was smoky and smelled of scorched flesh, whale oil and salt. Failure helped Lorna to drag Desi behind a large metal funnel, heaving and retching with pain. Once they were hidden from sight, Lorna wished them good luck and hurried away.

Only moments later, raised voices sounded in the room below and the roof door banged open. Failure fumbled in the backpack for the flare, as a dozen women and men spilled out onto the warm black felt.

"Hello, girl and boy," called the kidnapper in a sing song voice as the gang flanked him and began to inch forward. "We find you. No need to be scared. We sell you dead, we get nothing. Remember? We sell you good, we get good money, ok?"

Failure snapped the plastic cap from the body of the damp flare and ripped off the striker. Hands trembling, she scratched it across the igniter. Nothing happened.

A-gain, a-gain, her heart pounded. Failure dragged the striker across the igniter once more, but harder this time. It snapped in half.

"We brought you gift," the kidnapper called across the warm wind. He tossed something, which arced the length of the roof and came thudding down on the felt a few metres from Failure. It was the severed head of the ginger youth with the green serpent tattoos. He stared, upside down, at Failure in death.

Hey, that was my flare, the bloodshot eyes glared up at her.

Yeah, well you don't need it now, she replied, scraping the remaining half-striker once more against the igniter. This time, a hissing sounded, as the hidden combustibles within kicked into life. Failure thrust it skyward like a sword, as a fountain of vivid, neon pink light sprayed from the end of the flare. The sparks whooshed up into the darkness, a firework casting mad illuminations across the rooftop and up into the night and the city beyond. Shouts of alarm came from across the roof, where the gang halted in their tracks, their faces lit up like bonfire guys in the fierce, spitting glow. A hungry smile spread across the pink-lit face of the kidnapper, as gradually the flare puttered to a stop, plunging the night back into a homely gloom. Failure would die as she had lived; in the dark.

But then the door to the roof slammed open once more, spilling women and men in black uniforms into the slicing wind, like a herd of galloping black horses. Crossbow bolts were loosed and voices yelled in the night. The kidnappers turned and drew their weapons to fight, but they were outnumbered two to one, and the officers did not spare the bolts. The battle was over almost before it had begun, the greater number and superior weapons of the military officers overpowering the kidnappers like a tidal wave crushing a rowboat.

Stillness fell. Groans sounded in the night air. The formidable silhouette of Major Atsiler appeared in the roof doorway. She strode across the dead and the debris, dressed in her smart blue uniform, her long hair whipping in the high wind, an ice-cold expression in her eye.

Failure felt a warm current of relief thrum through her body. The sudden onset of security and safety was deafening, and it drew a blanket of deepest exhaustion over her. Failure allowed herself to collapse back on the felt.

Someone crouched beside her. A young man, with hair turning silver and his right arm suspended in a sling.

"But Smith died on the yacht," Failure told the night.

"Smith's alive and well," he replied. "My arm's not likely to be much use to me ever again, but I'm definitely alive."

Imagine how bad we look to him, the pocket watch ticked at Failure's chest. *The girl pale with exhaustion and a mangled leg; the boy half naked, face beaten, in a state of total collapse.*

Smith turned to a Private, calling, "Find something to use as a couple of stretchers over here, we're gonna need to carry them."

"Yeah, and get seaweed an all," Failure called. "Desi's got the water Blight. You need to get him some pulped up seaweed. As soon as possible."

On the far side of the roof, Atsiler had lined up the remaining members of the gang on their knees before her, their hands tied behind their backs. The kidnapper himself was amongst them, a crossbow bolt protruding from his thickly muscled shoulder, his jaw tensed in silent fury.

"Do they have Swift Courts in Norwich-on-Sea?" Failure asked Smith, as she and Desi were carried down through the building on makeshift stretchers.

"No need," Smith replied. "The Major is the law wherever she goes."

As they emerged from the sinking hospital, Failure heard a woman's voice singing an old sea shanty and glanced back to see. Up on the roof, the silhouetted figure of Major Atsiler caught Failure's eye. She was stood, her long hair dancing on the wind. Many stories beneath her, at the foot of the hospital, a dozen bodies were laid in a strange pile of twisted limbs, their hands still tied behind their backs. For the briefest of moments, the Major seemed to catch sight of Failure, then turned on her heel and vanished.

The yacht was humming to life as Failure and Desi were carried on board. Desi was whisked away, whilst Smith and another officer carried Failure to her cabin. After a short time, they were joined by a young woman with dark blonde hair, which was pulled back in a knot.

"Good evening, Failure," she said. "I'm Doctor Norwood, I'm here to take a look at your injuries."

"It's just my leg," Failure told her dismissively, "Are you the one looking after Desi too?"

"I am," the young woman nodded, kneeling beside the bed. She inspected the swollen mess between Failure's boot and shin.

"It looks like you've broken your ankle," the doctor mused quietly. "Nasty."

"Desi's in a much worse way than me, go and get him sorted first."

"Your friend is stable," the Doctor said. "But I need to re-set this ankle immediately, or you could lose your foot."

"Do you know what you're doing with the Blight?" Failure pressed her. "Have you already collected a bunch of seaweed? You need to mash it up and make a pulp and feed it to him. It draws out the poison. Returns the water to its own."

"Sounds like superstitious witchcraft," the doctor smiled, opening a medical bag and withdrawing a glass bottle of white powder.

"Have you seen what happens to a person, if the Blight takes them?" Failure asked.

The doctor paused for a split second, a glimmer of doubt in her brown eyes. "There haven't been any cases brought before the Kala's medical council," she said slowly. "The water sickness didn't exist before the Great Quake. Of course, we have heard rumours, from London Under mostly."

"Yeah, well the rumours are true," Failure insisted.

"Please take this," the doctor requested. "I'm going to put your ankle in a cast. But first, I need to reset it."

"Give him seaweed and fresh water, like I said," Failure pushed, taking the silver spoon and swallowing the foul, bitter white powder in one gulp. "It's that, or if you're the one looking after him, you're going to need an axe handy." A warmth and malaise began to flood Failure's bones and blood, making her heavy with sleep and entirely devoid of worry.

"How are you feeling after that bit of medicine, Failure?" The doctor asked.

"Like... I feel really goddam nice," Failure smiled stupidly, "Thanks doctor-doc."

"Superb. Officers, would you please help me by holding her still?"

"Yeah, hold me still, guys," Failure beamed. "I don't want to lose my lovely foot, after all. And I don't want Desi to die. I'm so glad Smith didn't die. I don't want doctor-doc to die, getting gobbled up. And I don't want you to die again, Smith," she smiled, as Smith pinned Failure's arms to her sides.

"This will only take a few moments," said the Doctor. "Don't bite your tongue."

"That's ok, I'm tough as hobnail boots." Failure grinned a wonky, self-congratulatory grin, then began to scream like a daemon in quicksand.

CHAPTER SEVENTEEN

The next morning, Failure woke to find that her ankle had been set in a heavy brown clay cast. The pain was almost gone and she was able to make her way out onto the blustery mid deck with the aid of the single crutch which had been left in her cabin.

She breathed in the fresh air, and soon after Major Atsiler joined her. "Good morning, Failure." Her expression was unusually blank and cold.

"How's Desi?" Failure demanded.

"He's alive. Doctor Norwood is very clever and sensible; she will be with him night and day until he recovers in full."

"I want to see him."

"It won't be necessary for you to visit Despair," the Major shook her head. "The last thing I need is you catching something, after all."

"You can't catch it," Failure protested. "You get it from the water."

"That has not been sufficiently tested to be safe. As such, I forbid you to visit him. Have you heard and understood that?"

Failure stared at the Major in the blinding white sunlight. There was something steely in that caring, handsome smile which Failure had been blind to before. Now she saw only the shadow cast by the pile of broken limbs at the base of the old hospital.

"It's very... it's been very convenient for you, Failure, all this," Atsiler mused. "It was Desi and not you who received a horrible beating to his face," the Major went on. "Desi who lost his valuable bird. Desi who fell sick. You escaped with nothing but a damaged ankle. It's almost as though the kidnappers didn't want you to get hurt."

"They didn't want either of us to get hurt," Failure retorted. "They said you'd pay for us if we were alive and well."

"That's interesting," Atsiler mused, "because we never received a ransom demand. Whoever they intended to sell you to, it was not us. Which was a big mistake."

"For them, clearly," Failure replied. "Especially given the way they died. Falling with their hands tied behind their backs."

"And if you have no idea who they were then why would that bother you in the least?"

"It's you who should be bothered," Failure told her. "It was a bad death. You've brought the shadow on yourself."

"Go back to your cabin, Failure," Atsiler snapped as she stalked away. "You're going to need your rest."

I told you their weapons had come from Pa, Failure's guts rolled. *He sent them after you. Maybe he was trying to rescue you?*

Funny way of rescuing someone, Failure shot back.

He's a funny kind of guy, her guts sighed. *Just don't tell Atsiler.*

I'm not telling that woman jack snap shut.

A shadow flickered overhead. Failure glanced up into the dazzling white light, shading her eyes. A large bird passed overhead, swooped and looped back, silhouetted against the morning sun. A flash of white plumage. A hint of yellow.

It can't be, her guts murmured. *It died on the banks of Norwich-on-Sea.*

And yet…

Failure turned her face up to the sunlight and closed her eyes. She raised her right arm out, just as she had seen him do. As though in answer, there was a whooshing and whistling of air. A heavy weight thudded down onto Failure's forearm. Two sets of sharp claws sank painfully around her flesh. Kezia was alert and calm, feathers unruffled. Failure laughed aloud and the vulture blinked back with her black eyes.

"Hello, stupid bird," Failure grinned, a tumult of joy boiling in her chest. "How in the world of mother goddess did you get here?

Come on, then. Let's find him together." Crutch in one hand, the glorious, ugly vulture perched on the other, Failure headed for the starboard promenade.

Every cabin door was locked but the last, the handle of which simply turned like a knife in butter, and Failure pulled it open, peering inside. Desi lay in the narrow bunk, pale as a corpse, his eyes closed. Doctor Norwood was sat in a chair beside him. As she turned to see the visitor, Failure saw doubt and fear in her sleep deprived features. Kezia launched herself from Failure's fist and flew across the cabin, landing on Desi's chest and nibbling at his lips and throat.

"What d'you think you're doing bringing that vermin in here?!" the doctor roared, her dark blonde hair escaping its knot, her grey eyes wild. She tried to grab at the vulture, shouting about hygiene and witchcraft and yokel magic, but was pecked and scratched in return until she gave up and sprinted out, screaming for help.

Failure knelt on the floor beside Desi's bed. On the cabinet beside him stood a glass bowl, full of a glutinous green mush. His lips were stained dark green.

"She's alive, Desi. Can you feel her standing on you?" Failure grinned. "It's Kezia. I don't know how, but she's here!"

Doctor Norwood returned with officers and orderlies, who piled in to the cabin, bustling and arguing, grabbing for the vulture, who flapped and clawed and evaded them all. A raging Atsiler followed, grabbing Failure by the neck of her sweater and pulling her away. Above the furore, the manic doctor began to shout. "He said something!" Her eyes were wild with hope. "He spoke. Everyone shut up, SHUT UP! What did you say, boy?"

It was little more than a weak murmur which came from the glimmer of a smile on Desi's green-stained lips. "Stupid bird."

The doctor burst into maniacal tears and laughter, forcing everyone out of the cabin with the strength of ten bears.

"From here on in you're confined to your cabin," Atsiler barked, as she marched Failure down the promenade. "And wipe that grin from your face."

Failure tried, but over the days that they sailed North, as she sat alone in her cabin, the grin shone beneath her black freckles like the brilliant radiance of the open sky.

PART TWO
THE ISLAND

CHAPTER EIGHTEEN

Days flowed together as the yacht ploughed its steady progress Northwards. Failure watched the world through the porthole, her nose pressed against the glass. Always the distant shore was in sight, speckled with its unfamiliar beaches and rivers and towns. Sometimes she caught sight of Kezia soaring through the skies above.

On the fifth day, as they passed the great fortress of Edinburgh Castle, perched high upon its cliff-top home, the doctor came to Failure's cabin.

"You're doing remarkably well," Norwood told her, a curious little frown upon her brow. "We'll try removing the cast tomorrow and give you a boot instead. Remarkably well."

That evening, as the sun fell low in the sky, Atsiler came to Failure's cabin and left her with a new set of clothes.

"Not long now," the Major had informed her. "You ought to look the part." So saying, she handed over a pair of black trainers, a pair of black shorts, and a grey t-shirt. The word 'Fitznil' had been embroidered onto the back of the shirt in black thread.

"What's Fitznil mean?" Failure asked.

"It's the surname which polite society gives to children without surnames. You will go by Failure Fitznil."

That night, Failure leaned out of the stifling cabin into the fresh salt breeze and saw stars for the first time in her life; millions of pinpricks of disarming, brilliant silver lights; precious jewels twinkling and dazzling above.

Stars are nice, aren't they? the pocket watch thrummed at her chest.

They are, Failure sighed. *What's the 'but' I can sense coming?*

But there's something else you could sit and stare at tonight, isn't there? If you can't sleep.

The letter that Pa gave you, her guts cut in.

Failure pulled herself back into the cabin and, in the glow of fireflies and twinkling stars, took out the snakeskin wallet and turned it over in her hands.

This is something about your mother, her guts squirmed. *You might learn something about her.*

Like a time traveller, the pocket watch ticked.

Like a ghost, her guts corrected.

What are you waiting for?

Failure drew out the handful of papyrus sheets from within and sat cross-legged on her bed.

What if it's something... she paused. *What if it's something sad. Disappointing. What if it's something that says she didn't want me. What if it's about her murder? What if it was somehow... you know...*

Go on, her heart thumped.

You know, Failure replied.

Your fault, her heart thudded. Her throat tightened.

Only one way to find out, her guts resolved. Failure took a deep breath and looked down at the top page. It was dated November, fifteen years before.

To my own one. Failure. There is so much to explain and I don't have long. I will try and give you what I can here, because my precious little one, you are going to face so much. I am already so proud of you, and you are so young. I long to stay with you. But I can't. It would place you in so much danger that I don't have any choice.

So she was already planning to leave you, before she was murdered? Failure guts rumbled.

It doesn't make any sense, Failure thought back.

Keep on, read more, her heart urged.

I want to explain the beginning of you. First, then; your father. I met him when I was serving my five years in conscription. We served as orderlies in the Old Med refugee camp on the Isle of Wight. He was a career soldier, destined to go to the front after our service together, and I had a place at a university. So, our time together was very sweet but very brief.

There you are, then, Failure's guts interrupted her again. *A career soldier, so he's most likely dead anyway.*

This is exactly why I've always said that we shouldn't get our hopes up about things, Failure sighed.

Read more, Failure's heart reminded her and again she turned back to the page.

After conscription, I took my place at university in Oxford, to study Earth Sciences. Geology. Rocks are like maps of time and past events, written into the earth. A different kind of time travel. I was obsessed with my work and studied late into the evenings. It was on one of those evenings, when I was alone in the lab, that Professor Tomas Peterson, the head of Earth Sciences at that time, came into the department in a great hurry. He explained that he had received an urgent summoning from the Barons and had to depart that very moment on an expedition. He had been told to bring with him an assistant. I dropped what I was doing and followed him—

A rapid knock sounded at the door to Failure's cabin. She crossed the room on bare feet and opened the door. Instead of the guard normally stationed there, it was Desi. Grinning. Failure pulled him inside, closing the door behind him with a quiet click. He was dressed in the same grey t-shirt and black shorts as she was, his Triumph tattoos performing a colourful dance across his skin; a running wolf, a chalice, a flame, the Goddess' raised hands, an oak tree. His eyes were bright and conker brown once more. For the first time, Failure wondered how she looked in his eyes;

wild mane of tangled ash coloured hair and pale, burned, sun starved skin. She felt bottomlessly shy. They stood across from one another, stuck in a sudden void of words.

"I'm not meant to go outside after dark," Desi whispered, at the same moment as Failure said, "How did you get past the guards? Sorry," she laughed quietly, "You go first."

"They told me you were restricted to your cabin," Desi said in a hushed voice. "But the handover always takes a few minutes, and the young guy with the grey hair is about to come on shift for your door. I saw him right on the other side of the yacht, so I guessed I could just about make it before him. I'm meant to stay inside, but I need to ask you something."

"Well, you're technically inside now," Failure said, her skin humming. "And I haven't left my cabin. So, neither of us are actually breaking the rules."

Desi shook his head and laughed quietly. His lips were tinged green from the seaweed medicine. She felt, for the first time in her life, that she was part of a clan. It felt better than the hiss and blush of lichen tox.

"What will they do to you at the Programme for running away?" She asked, but before the words had died on her breath, he interrupted her, saying, "There's no time for all that, I just wanted to know; how did you find her?"

"Kezia?"

He nodded a single, quick nod.

"Well, I didn't really," Failure murmured, thinking back to the sun-blazed moment on the deck when Kezia had soared above her. "She found me. I was on the deck. I held my hand out to her and she came and landed on me. I guess she must have followed our every step since the kidnappers scared her off. Not such a stupid bird after all."

"She doesn't go to anyone else," Desi whispered. The grin had faded from his face, his eyes bright, curious, searching in the firefly glow. Failure felt her burned skin, scarlet under his gaze.

"She only comes to me. Why did she go to you?"

Failure made no reply. Instead, she stepped forward at the same moment as he did. And this time their kiss was one of sinking worlds and skies so clear you could see burning balls of gas dying in other lifetimes. Failure's heart raced painfully, as though it would hammer itself out of her chest. She pressed herself against the wall of Desi's body, and heard the call of his own heart, hammering back in answer.

Then came a banging on the cabin door. "It's Smith," came a deep voice from the other side. Failure and Desi sprang apart, mirroring one another's horrified expressions. "The boy needs to get back to his cabin right now. We're arriving at Eylan Morr."

CHAPTER NINETEEN

The craggy facade of the island's south coast rose before them like a shattered cathedral. Failure stood between Major Atsiler and Desi on the blustery deck of a small landing boat which picked its way deftly through waves and the rocks, under the glaring heat of the sun.

The female crew of the lander wore long brown dresses with white frill collars, high brown boots, their hair cropped close to their skulls. Each of them was armed with military grade crossbows.

"Who're the Guzzers in the fancy brown dresses?" Failure shouted to Atsiler above the roar of the water while grabbing the handrail, unsteady on her protective boot.

"Governesses, not guards," the Major corrected in a shout. "They look after the pastoral needs of the students and the day-to-day running of the Programme. Maintenance, laundry, cooking, that sort of thing."

"They cook with crossbows?" Failure asked, but her voice was lost on the wind.

Crossing the black sandy beach, they ascended the cliff up a rough rock stairway in single file, like a line of worker ants, Kezia swooping above them on the hot winds. At the summit was an enormous black metal fence, ten feet high, its upper rim twisted into sharp, curved barbs. Failure took a deep breath and glanced back at the world behind. Then she climbed the last three, two, one steps and passed through an open doorway.

The world beyond was a vast, open plateau. Flat and broad and baking under a piercing white sky. Flanking Failure to her left and right were six white stone statues on black marble bases, through which they must pass to enter the island. Each statue depicted one of the successful Time Corp Travellers, posed in different depictions of glory, arms raised to the sky or else held out wide, or shading their eyes to see far into the distance. Their stone faces were chiselled into expressions of ecstasy and cries of euphoria.

A white pathway led across the centre of the plateau, carving it in half like a backbone, leading to two enormous black glass buildings. The larger was spiked and angular, towering up into the sky like a jagged mountain. The smaller was a dome of enormous black glass hexagons, so reminiscent of a giant insect's lair that Failure's skin crawled. Beyond the plateau and the black fence which surrounded it, the island rolled away for miles, and the lonely tip of a lighthouse, striped in white and red, was just visible in the vivid, hazy dawn. Beyond, and on all sides, was the sparkling sea.

Stood in formation across the grand plateau were the students of the Royal Scottish Time Programme. They faced forwards in perfect lines, the wind whipping their hair and stirring their clothes. Not one of them moved a muscle. Their feet were planted shoulder width apart. One hand tucked behind the back. The other neatly propped on a hip. Each student wore the same grey and black uniform. Their gleaming, bare limbs were inked with Triumph badges, making Failure feel strangely naked before them.

These students were nothing like the people Failure had known in her lifetime; glowing skin in the place of pox scars and pallor; athletic and lithe bodies, without bowed and broken bones from lack of sunlight; lustrous, clean hair in the place of lice, plaits and shaved heads; expressions alert and interested and open, not sunken with mistrust, disquiet and desperation.

A horn blared out, shattering the silence. Every student raised the hand from their hip to a perfect right angle in front of the body, a single finger pointing upwards, sending their luck to the Kala. Failure instinctively raised her own right hand and forefinger in response.

A woman approached along the white pathway. She wore a dark green skirt suit and brown fur bolero, walking with a swish on black high heeled shoes. Every step she took was striking, a dart meeting its target. Her lips were painted dark purple, her hair coiled in a golden turban. From a distance she looked young but close up Failure saw that she was closer to sixty than twenty. The woman greeted Major Atsiler with a firm handshake.

"This is Don Zoya," Atsiler called to Failure over the hot, whipping wind. "The Deputy Headmistress of the Royal Scottish Time Programme. Don, you know Despair already, of course. And this is your new recruit; Failure Fitznil."

"Perfection," Don Zoya said in a rich, husky voice. "Let's get up to the main building for the Headmaster's morning address. Come." She turned on her polished heels and beat a march between the six white statues. Failure followed along the backbone path, between endless rows of students.

You know what they see? her guts asked. *Because of that ankle? That you were weak.*

No, they see that you heal, the pocket watch corrected. *They see that you're a fighter.*

They passed the black insect-lair dome and emerged from the grid of students at the facade of the main building. Grotesque, sun-damaged stone gargoyles crouched on the many spires and apexes, dripping with sea spray as though dribbling. From the tallest tower, a black and gold flag bearing the Time Corp symbol slapped back and forwards in the ferocious wind. A series of ten-foot-high brass letters glinted like real gold in the searing sunlight, spelling out, "Fortiter ire retro".

That's what's written on the face of our pocket watch, her guts thrummed. Failure's heart thundered like wildfire. *The same. The same. The same.*

What does it say? Failure demanded of the watch. But it could only tick back frantically where it hung at her breast.

A few paces ahead, Desi held out his arm and made a fist. For a mad moment, bred into her by a violent childhood, Failure expected Desi to punch Madame Zoya. But instead, Kezia swooped down and landed upon his fist without a sound.

With a grinding of stone upon stone, a thick white pillar began to rise from the earth beside them, creating a high, exposed platform. A set of stairs was carved in a spiral fashion around it, and a young gentleman climbed them to stand atop the pillar. He was tall and thin, dressed in a three-piece tweed suit, with greying brown hair, a neatly trimmed moustache and thin wire spectacles. Woven around his neck like a silken scarf was the skin of a snake, stuffed and treated so that its dry scales gleamed in the bright sunlight. A static buzz winced across the plateau, as electronic speakers were switched into life by an unseen hand.

"Students, teachers and staff," the Headmaster began. "Good morning. I would like to begin with the announcement of this week's Star Pupils. Pride Kingsly and Negligence Lawrence. Congratulations. You will of course both receive your messages from home today as your reward. In other news, we are delighted to welcome Mr Despair LeoMontague back to the Programme after his brief absence. We also welcome our new pupil, Failure Fitznil, to our community. Welcome, Failure; may you go bravely in the past."

"GO BRAVELY IN THE PAST," chanted hundreds of voices in response.

"Failure is the first ever pupil to join us from London Under. Please do your best to welcome her and assist her in whatever she needs. And finally, I have a very important announcement to make; in four days' time, we will attempt our next Travelling."

A ripple of gasps passed across the plateau like a forest fire. When silence had fallen once again, the Headmaster continued from atop the high pillar.

"Two students will be selected from amongst your number and given their chance to make history. If successful, they will become our seventh and eighth Travellers. We will be utilising

Conductor IV, along with all of the alterations made since the unsuccessful attempt in September. As is traditional, the evening of the attempt will be marked with a formal dance, where you will be encouraged to enjoy yourselves responsibly. But before that, it is time to apply yourselves like you never have before. Let's get to work."

CHAPTER TWENTY

"Good luck, Failure," Atsiler called after Failure in a quiet voice, as Zoya led her through the front doors, and Desi filed away with the other students. "And remember what I told you."

"You told me a lot of things," Failure called back, thinking once more of the pile of bodies at the foot of the sinking hospital.

"The faculty of the Royal Scottish Time Programme," Madame Zoya called to Failure as they entered the black glass entrance hall, gesturing to dozens of grand, colourful portraits which adorned the walls. "Every researcher, teacher and mechanic who has been a part of this glorious endeavour. And of course you will recognise our Travellers. Darkness Jones. Shame Sandu. Penitence Morton. Reckless O'Neill. Penitence McCleod. Futility Watanabe." Madame Zoya spoke each name with reverence. "Perhaps one day your own image will join them. Imagine that. Follow me, we'll go straight up to the Parade in the lift. I want to show you the grounds."

They travelled upwards in a small, mirrored lift and emerged into open air at the very summit, where the wind was fierce and cool. A long walkway stretched away in both directions like the battlements of a castle. Below was an internal courtyard which comprised a running track and assault course.

"This is the parade," Madame Zoya called above the wind. "Students are not normally permitted up here, as our student's safety is our highest priority. But I wanted to show you a couple of things. Firstly, the Perimeter."

Madame Zoya gestured to the high, barbed black fence which surrounded the compound. "It marks the extremes of the Programme grounds," she went on. "Students are forbidden to cross it. The island beyond is not safe. Cliff corrosion, landslides, bogs as deadly as quicksand, not to mention the native wildlife. The courtyard down there is where you will have daily Drill," Zoya continued, "although I believe you will be excused that pleasure until your ankle is fully healed. You can better use your time in the library, which you will find in the basement. You may enjoy the grounds within the Perimeter as you see fit, and all students are permitted to worship at the Ring, when accompanied by a teacher on an authorised visit."

"What's the Ring?" Failure asked.

"Have a look out there, to the East of the Island," Madame Zoya replied, "and tell me what you see."

"A lot of grass," Failure said, holding her long fair hair back from her freckled face and peering across sunbaked hills, scrub, rock and rivulet. "Some old fallen down buildings. And..." Her gaze settled on a valley, in which stood a great ring of standing stones. Gleaming in the sunlight, as though they had stood there since the dawn of time. Twice the height of a person, there were fifteen of them, arranged like the broken teeth of a giant.

"And some big old stones," Failure breathed.

"Yes, you will learn more about them in your Anchors class," Madame Zoya replied. "Along with Quantum Mechanics, Latitude and Longitude, Dead Reckoning, Drill, Dimensions, General Relativity, BioMatter, Faith Meditation, String theory and Dark Matter."

"Do we learn anything in that language written on the front of the main building?" Failure asked. "Cos, I don't even know what that language is."

"It's Latin," Madame Zoya replied. "You have a lot of catching up to do. You see the building there," she gestured out across the plateau to the gleaming black glass dome. "That dome houses the Conductor. It is our secret weapon against time. Our greatest achievement. It is from within that building that six young people have travelled. Can you imagine, Failure, getting the opportunity to travel back to another time? To right the wrongs of the past. It is a promise of hope from the Goddess. It is an honour. You are very precious to us, all of you. Now then, I must introduce you to your guide. First, however, I will need to confiscate your watch." Her voice was like a dead weight in the breeze.

"I don't wear a watch," Failure lied.

"I can see that you don't wear a wristwatch," Madame Zoya smiled. "But I'm talking about whatever it is upon your person that is ticking."

Failure felt her heart sink into the very pit of her stomach.

Madame Zoya held out her hand. "All of your personal possessions should have been confiscated before you stepped foot on this island. Hand it over." Zoya said, wiggling the fingers of her outstretched hand. Seeing no alternative, Failure slipped her fingers around the chain at her neck and lifted it over her head. The chain pulled the pocket watch out from its concealed place by her heart. It felt like she was giving away her own tongue. Zoya took the watch in her hand with an unreadable expression. "This item is made of gold," she said coldly.

"You're kidding me?" Failure exclaimed. "Real gold? I could've got a small fortune for that in London Under, north bank or south. I've been wearing it for weeks; thought it was a goddam bit of tin junk. You wanna buy it off me?"

"The trading of gold is illegal," Madame Zoya snapped, with no hint of amusement in the painted lines of her face. "Where did you come by it?"

"It was inside a bomb," Failure replied truthfully. "One I nicked fair and square."

Don't let me go, Failure heard the fluttering tick of the watch.

"I will be delivering this directly to the Headmaster," Zoya went on. "We need all the gold we can get."

Don't let me— the Professor slipped the watch into her pocket, and the sound was gone.

Poor old ticker, her guts sighed.

How did Madame Zoya hear it ticking? Failure asked.

I have no idea, her guts rumbled. *Maybe I wasn't the old ticker's best friend, but it was ours. They stole it from us.*

They did.

They're going to melt it down for gold.

They're going to pay, Failure vowed.

That's what you said about Pa, her guts sighed.

CHAPTER TWENTY-ONE

On their return to the entrance hall, Failure and Madame Zoya were met by a girl in uniform. Her radiant, golden-brown skin was adorned with a slew of Triumphs; the Goddess; a grandfather clock; Saturn; an ocean under a full moon. She was tall and athletic, with a mass of gleaming corkscrew black curls tied on top of her head. She looked like she could run a marathon, then kill a Sylkie at the end of it. At her ankles, a small, furry tiger cub padded about, nuzzling her with its button brown nose and spiky whiskers. The extraordinary pair were linked by a chain, which ran from the silver collar around the tiger's neck to a brown leather belt around the girl's waist.

"Failure, this is one of our star pupils, Doom Van DeLey. Doom is a fellow first-year student, who will show you to your dorm. If you work hard and follow the example of students like her then who knows how far you could go."

Madame Zoya's high heels clicked away on the marble floor, leaving Failure and Doom alone.

"So… that's a tiger," Failure said, eyeing the creature nervously.

"Her name is Kimsha," the girl said, no hint of good humour on her beautiful face. "She's my anchor. I'll show you the dorms while everyone's getting sorted after morning Drill. This way."

Failure followed Doom and the tiger cub up a sweeping marble staircase and through a series of corridors, which became increasingly austere the further they passed from the grand entrance hall.

"Hey, you know the boy Desi who arrived with me today?" Failure asked, struggling to keep up with Doom on her cumbersome boot. "Will they punish him? You know, for running away?"

"I have no idea," Doom replied, not looking back, pushing open a doorway. "And I couldn't care less. This is the East Wing. It's mostly just dorms and mess spaces. You're in dorm seven."

In the corridor beyond, they were met with a wall of noise and a cloud of billowing steam; chatter, laughter, footsteps, running water, the smell of sweat and soap. Dozens of bunk rooms branched off the corridor, full of narrow beds and gleaming bodies. Students milled about, leaning in doorways, chatting on bunks, using doorframes for pull-ups, spraying themselves with potions and spritzes, packing bags and styling hair. As Failure passed, the unfamiliar name *Fitznil* reverberated around her like a dark mantra, sometimes in brazen comments, sometimes in scurrying whispers.

You're like an exhibit in a travelling freak show, her guts whispered, burying themselves deep inside.

I don't give a god damn, Failure replied. *I just want to get my goddam watch back before its melted.*

You should hide the letter Pa gave you too, her guts warned. *What if they try and take that too? What if there's something dangerous in it? You should have read it all on the yacht and got rid of it. You were scared to read it and it made you slow.*

Jack-Snap-Shut-Up, Failure thought back, knowing the guts were always right.

"This is Dorm seven," Doom said, turning into a bunk room. The students within fell silent, fractious electricity in the air, ready to sting. Half a dozen eyes homed in on Failure like heat-seeking harpoons.

"That's your bunk up there, above Darkness," Doom said, gesturing to an upper bunk in the centre of the room. A student with long brown hair and painted lips was lying on the lower bunk, reading a book. He peeked around the corner of it, smiled and said, "She's a lot smaller than I'd imagined."

Failure clambered up the ladder to her own bunk and thought longingly of her stuffy attic bedroom at home; her little iron framed bed and blankets; her Zeeva stowed under the mattress; her trinkets and steals perched on the sloped windowsill in the eaves; the lock on the door and the view over the river. Pa had sometimes come and sat on the mattress beside her, worrying and wondering and regretting drinking it all away. Whenever Winston had left him again, he would sleep on her floor, like a terrified child.

Was that weird as well? her guts asked her, as Failure surveyed her new bedroom. *You can't imagine Desi's dad crying himself to sleep on his floor, can you?*

It just made him feel better, Failure replied. *And Pa wasn't my dad. My dad was some squaddie. And he didn't even know I existed.*

"Hey, Doom, did you see Desi yet?" A tall, blonde boy stood leaning on the doorframe. He was tanned and handsome.

"Nope," Doom replied, from where she was re-tying her hair.

"What d'you think they'll do to him?" The blonde boy went on, with an amused smirk.

"Whatever they do, Pride," Doom replied, lifting her tiger cub, which growled deep within its throat, "it's absolutely none of my business. And when you see him, you can tell him that from me."

Pride whistled and chuckled, and some kind of ripple seemed to pass through the dorm, which Failure could feel but not understand.

"But congratulations on the star pupil recognition this week," Doom added, going to the blonde boy and shaking his hand firmly. "Good timing for you as well, right before the next travelling. Well done."

"Thanks," Pride beamed, "but don't try and change the subject. Hey, new girl: Fitznil, isn't it? Do you know where they sent my boy Desi?" A small group was crowding in behind the boy at the doorway now.

"I dunno Jack-Snap-Shut," Failure replied from atop her bunk. A titter of giggles passed amongst the crowd.

"Ah well, he's a trooper," Pride grinned carelessly, moving aside to allow a girl to pass him and enter the room. She had ink black, short, cropped hair and large, blue, heavily lidded eyes, which gave her the appearance of a wizened owl, old before its years. She used two crutches to walk and, though her arms and shoulders were lean and muscular, she was petite and slight.

"He'll be fine," Pride was saying. "So, what's your story? Did you know you're sort of famous here? We thought you were gonna turn up with a third eye or wings or something."

"The rumour is that she's claiming she can cause a time mirage without an Anchor," said the girl on the crutches. "Which isn't possible. And given she can't possibly have an anchor yet; something doesn't add up."

"Well, you guys know more than me," Failure shrugged.

"The point is that if you're saying you made a time mirage happen," the girl pressed on, "then you're either some kind of mutant, or some kind of trickster, or some kind of liar."

The curious crowd watched like a pack of hyenas, gradually closing in on a cold desert night.

"So, what is it?" the black-haired girl insisted, smirking. "Mutant, trickster or liar? I know where my money's going."

"Why would I tell you a goddam thing about my life?" Failure shot at her.

"No need to be shy," the girl sneered. "We just want to know where we stand."

"Who's 'we'?" The blonde-haired boy Pride called from where he still leaned in the doorway. "Don't embarrass yourself trying to make us all into one big knot, Torment. Just because there's a new freak in town doesn't suddenly make you one of us."

"I'd rather drown than be one of you," she spat back, at which Pride laughed.

"We need to go to Quantums," Doom called up to Failure. "And you can stop winding her up, Torment," she added to the petite girl.

"Why d'you care?" the girl smirked. "From what I understand she's the last person in the world that you would want to protect."

"A Travelling's in the offing," Doom snapped. "I intend to be chosen, so I'm not keen on getting a black mark by my name thanks to fighting in my dorm."

"Don't worry about Princess Try-hard," Torment sneered, turning back to Failure. Her expression was expectant and hungry, as were the dozen others who watched with the same appetite. "Worry about trying to explain yourself."

"What's got you by the throat?" Failure asked, her skin starting to prickle with aggravation.

"You've got no idea what the rest of us went through to be here," Torment snarled. "No idea what we've sacrificed and risked and given. And here you waltz in with a fancy story and a free pass."

"A lot of people are going to be jealous of you, Failure," Doom cut in. "But it doesn't have to be personal. Ignore her."

"No one here is jealous," Torment snapped, a little too forcefully. "But she should have had to go through the selection, so she was here on merit, like the rest of us."

"Pretty ironic coming from you," Pride chipped in from the doorway. "Given that the rest of us passed the *entire* selection process. Including the physicals. If anyone got a free pass, it was you." So saying, he gave the doorframe a jaunty thump and sauntered away.

"Come on, let's go," Doom said, as students began grabbing sweatshirts and bags and heading out, responding to some unseen change of the tide that Failure didn't understand. But Torment was stock still, her heart-shaped face flushed deepest red and crumpled in fury. Her blue eyes clamped on Failure. "Can you do it, or not? Failure."

"What do you shoulder?" Failure asked, climbing down the bunk as ripples of anger sizzled across her skin like electric currents.

"You've already heard them using my name," the girl sneered as they came face to face. "I hope you aren't gonna try and form a knot with me. Because we heard that's what you already tried with Desi. Embarrassingly for you."

"Shut your ne'er-do-well mouth," Failure heard herself saying. "I don't give a goddamn about knots or whatever. This is London Under code of honour. We like to formally exchange names before knocking someone out."

"Well then, I shoulder the Torment."

"Nice to meet you, Torment. I shoulder the Failure," Failure snarled, and the next moment launched herself toward the girl. Strong arms wrapped around Failure and pulled her back and away. She fought, but the arms were stronger.

"Alright that's enough," Doom was shouting in Failure's ear. Failure struggled on briefly against the girl's vicelike grip, before falling still. The remaining students were staring at Failure aghast, a mingled collective expression of disgust and shock on their faces. Doom let Failure go, saying, "It's time for everyone to go. Hang around another minute and you'll be late for class."

Torment gave Failure a final look of disgust, but slunk away smoothly on her crutches, breaking the tension and causing the other students to quickly melt away. Her heart racing, Failure climbed the ladder back up to her bunk as quickly as the boot on her ankle would allow.

What were you thinking? her guts demanded. *Fighting doesn't count as staying under the radar.*

She was baiting me, Failure muttered. *If I hadn't done it, they'd have seen me as weak.*

Yeah, well now they'll see you as something worse than that, her guts replied.

Good, Failure growled.

"I'll wait outside for one minute, then I'm gone," Doom called up to Failure, exiting the dorm. Finding herself alone at last, Failure drew the snakeskin wallet from her pocket and slipped it swiftly beneath the pillow on her bed. But as she did so, the backs of her fingers brushed against a cold fragment of papyrus.

Failure froze. She drew it out. Written on the papyrus in untidy black ink were the words, '*If you want your watch back, come to the lighthouse tomorrow night after dark.*'

You've been told to keep your head down, her guts rumbled. *Or you're gonna be kicked out and thrown to the Swift Courts. Rip that message up and forget it ever existed.*

I saw the lighthouse when we arrived, Failure breathed silently. *Somewhere off on the other side of the island.*

That watch isn't worth it, her guts protested. *It's just a watch. This is trouble, which you're meant to be staying out of. And what about The Perimeter?* her guts raced on.

It's just a wall, Failure grinned. *What's a wall between friends?*

Well, it's a wall, her guts replied. *Which is massive and spiked and patrolled by armed guards.*

I don't like the idea of trying to scale it, Failure mused back. *I'm not a bad climber, but that thing's been designed to rip you to shreds at the top. Can't burrow under it, it must be sunk in meters of concrete. And there's no going around a complete ring. I'll just have to find a way through it.*

CHAPTER TWENTY-TWO

Failure joined Doom in the corridor and once again followed in her wake, amongst the throngs of students heading for their lessons.

"This morning is double BioMatter," Doom explained. "And this is your timetable." She passed a small booklet back to Failure. "There's a map of the Programme on the back that should get you around from this afternoon onwards."

"Ok thanks," Failure said, taking the booklet, whilst tearing the note to shreds in her pocket with the other hand. "And thanks for your help with that girl Torment. Probably shouldn't get in a fight on my first morning. Desi said I just have to keep my head down and avoid the ghosts and I'll be fine. Is it true, about the island ghosts? Something about a haunted lighthouse?" As she spoke, Failure scattered the shreds of the note like breadcrumbs along the heaving corridors.

Doom paused and looked back at Failure with beautiful, deep brown eyes. "Look, I might as well be honest from the start and say that just because we share a dorm room, and because I was asked to show you around, that doesn't make us friends."

A titter of laughter came from the small knot of students who were following close behind.

"Yeah, fine, I was just wondering about the ghosts," Failure shrugged, though the laughter felt like surprisingly painful pricks of glass on the skin. "We have a lot of ghosts where I'm from, so I wondered if the lighthouse was—"

"I know that you nearly got Desi killed," Doom cut in, and for the first time that day, her glossy and impeccable exterior wavered, as though Failure were seeing the same image through a tear in the eye. But there was nothing sentimental in the crack of Doom's cool facade. Beneath was a molten core of repressed rage.

"I know you kissed him. When he was half-dead. Which is forbidden, by the way. And could have got him into even more trouble than he's already in."

"I don't… what are you talking about?" Failure faltered, feeling sick to her stomach.

"He wrote to me by pigeon when you were still on the journey," Doom replied, taking a deep breath and gradually sealing the crack in her facade with brutal cheer. "If anything had happened to him, it would have been your fault."

"No, it would have been his fault for running away in the first place," Failure shot back. "And he's lucky I haven't ripped his sneakthief face off for writing to people about me behind my back. We don't do that where I'm from."

"One can only imagine where you're from," Doom smiled.

"The trouble for people who blush easily like you do," Failure said, "is that all the stuff you're thinking gets written on your skin in blood. Like now. When you're trying to be calm, but actually boiling over with jealousy."

Doom laughed a tinkling bell of a laugh, then leaned in close to Failure and hissed, "Jealous of you? Ragged hair like a village witch. Filthy nails like you've been digging up graves. And Goddess knows what possesses a person to paint their lips green." She stood back to her full height and said, "I hope that's all clear for you, Failure. Let's get to BioMatter."

Failure followed Doom to a large outdoor quad, surrounded by tall concrete walls, which were lined with dozens of cages. The concrete floor was wet, as though it had recently been hosed down, and it sloped into the centre, where the last of the water rivulets ran down into a grill. A woman with vivid purple hair and large, red-framed glasses, wearing a white lab coat, was awaiting the students as they gathered.

The boy with the painted lips and sly smile from the dorms crossed to Failure and spoke in a quiet voice. "That's Madame Flowers. And I'm your bunkmate. I shoulder the Darkness," he held a finger to the air, sending his luck to the Kala. "But everyone calls me Ness. Enjoying your welcome to the Time Programme? Lessons. Students. Time Travel. All the usual stuff."

"Give me a bare-knuckle fight or a flood Sylkie and I'm good," Failure muttered. "I don't think I'll be very good at being a kid in a school."

"Well, then we have one thing in common," Ness smiled. "I've never been good at being a kid in school, and I've been doing it since I was five."

"Alright, students," Madame Flowers called, pushing her glasses higher on the bridge of her long nose, her violet eyes flashing with a lusty thrill. "Choose an occupant of a cage and start making your own notes. We'll begin reviewing in twenty minutes."

"Don't you worry about Doom Van DeLey," Ness said quietly, as the two of them walked to a cage on the far side of the quad. "Her bark is worse than her bite."

"I don't worry about anyone," Failure replied. "And my bite's worse than my bark."

"Well, that's good then," Ness went on, smiling. "Because you're going to need your wits about you. Nothing's quite what it seems, here at the good old Time Programme. Anyway, seeing as we're bunk mates, I guess it's time I offered you my services. I'm a good person to know if you need sorting out with anything, if you know what I mean? Are you planning on joining a knot?"

"What is this knot thing?" Failure asked. "Where I come from knots are for tying up boats and prisoners."

"It means a sort of alliance," Ness explained, as they wandered along the rows of cages, some of which were empty, some of which contained animals and insects. "Like a friendship, but more formal. They're actually forbidden, but it's going on under the surface, like everything else. Word to the wise, it puts you at a real disadvantage, if you don't find one."

They arrived at the far end of the quad, where a large cage lay in shadow. No other students were crowded around its bars.

"Is it true, what they're saying about you?" Ness asked, joining her in the shade.

"I don't even know what a time mirage is," Failure sighed, "so I have no idea if I caused one and frankly—"

"No, sorry," Ness interrupted, "I meant, is it true that you kissed Desi? I suppose he thought it was better to just confess it straight away than to wait."

"What d'you mean, confess it?" Failure asked.

"Oh, didn't he tell you?" Ness responded, biting his lower lip, with a poorly-concealed grin and rolling his eyes. "That's so typical of him. They have a thing, Desi and Doom. I mean they obviously don't. Officially. Because that's forbidden. But they can't stay away from each other. It's been going on since the very start of Selection."

Failure felt her heart try to bury itself in her guts. Across the quad, in the sunshine, Doom Van DeLey was laughing with the purple haired teacher, sipping a bottle of water as though it were champagne.

"I guess I put a spanner in the works," Failure said, trying to sound bold and careless.

"Not the first spanner," Ness said with a raised eyebrow. "But that's Desi, ain't it? So don't forget. Anything you need that you can't get out in the open, you come to me." He turned to walk away.

"Hey Ness, wait a second," Failure called after him. "What's the price? I mean, just in case I do need you; what do you trade for?"

Ness smiled, inclining his head and pursing his painted lips. "Hmmm," he mused. "It's different for everyone. But for you... I'd trade with you for... for your secrets, I think. Just come and find me, any time."

Failure turned back to the cage and peered into the darkness. There was a shuffling of claws on concrete. The creature within the enclosure came closer. Its breath was rasping and smelled putrid. It was an odour she had smelt before. Creature flesh and fur. Musky and bloody and salty and stale. A pair of bright orange eyes blinked, and Failure saw a sheen of golden fur and black scale. Her blood seemed to run cold in her veins.

"How've they got one of you in there?" she breathed at the creature. "Such a long way from home?"

In the shadows beyond there was a flick of tail and a whimper.

Of course he has a girlfriend, Failure's guts told her with no little anger. *Why wouldn't he? It's not like you made some kind of agreement. You just saved each other. And kissed. It was just something that happened.*

I wish he hadn't told her, her guts murmured, feeling hollow. *That girl... she's like... she's like a goddess. And we're a... a...* her guts searched in their hollowness for the answer, which came at last from the heart. *We're just a spanner.*

We're not just a spanner, Failure insisted. *He only told her about the first kiss. He didn't tell her about the other one. In the cabin. He's kept that between the two of us, at least.*

That was only this morning, her guts sighed. *The only reason he didn't tell her about that was because he hasn't had the time.*

Look, just because I haven't done this before doesn't mean that I don't know what I'm doing now, Failure thought back determinedly. *And besides all this, I need to get past the perimeter so I can meet whoever has my watch. And I need to read my letter before I get searched and get that stolen too.*

What about me? her heart thudded.

You were better off when you were nothing but an early warning system, Failure snapped. *I suggest you go back to that.*

"And as for you," Failure breathed aloud to the monster in the cage. "I wonder who you were, before the blight. Before you changed."

A pair of amber eyes flashed at her from the shadows, then drew away into the darkness.

CHAPTER TWENTY-THREE

After an afternoon blur of classes that she couldn't understand and kids she understood even less, Failure snuck into the grand entrance hall and waited for quiet.

This is a terrible idea, her guts chided as Failure pressed the button inside the lift marked 'parade.'

Yeah well, I need to be on my own to read the goddam letter, Failure replied silently. *So shut it.*

The night air of the Parade was hot and humid, the black sky above winking with the light of millions of stars. Failure imagined that same sky peering down over the same waves when all of the land was gone. The moon would glow in the reflected light of the sun. The waves would roll and recede in response to the moon's pull. Time wouldn't really exist by then, when there was no one left to count it. She squeezed her eyes shut and hissed, "Wait!" at the sea. But the waves rolled on with a hush and a shush, whispering, *That's not how it works.*

I know, I know, her heart beat back.

Looking out over Eylan Tor, Failure could see the tip of the ancient, crumbling lighthouse in the distance.

It's not that far, she told her guts. *Tomorrow night we have to be there. That gives us a whole day to make a plan.*

You and your plans, her guts sighed.

Failure clambered alongside one of the ugly stone gargoyles who lined the path. She took out the snakeskin wallet and withdrew its precious contents.

My mother was about to go on a trip somewhere with that Professor, Failure reminded her guts. *Let's see where she went.*

Failure unfolded the pages and moved them an inch out of the shadow and into the moonlight, which shone now upon the black ink writing.

Peterson and I were marched out of the University by two military officers, and driven to RAF Brize Norton, where a small plane was awaiting us. Peterson explained what little he knew. That there was a British-led dig happening in the Arctic. Headed up by Dr Rosalie LeoSirus; a brilliant explorer and archaeologist, the best there was. Driven. Ruthless sometimes, he said. That was the first I ever heard of Dr Rosalie LeoSirus.

Don't we know that name from somewhere? Failure's guts wondered.

I don't know... Failure paused, frowning. The three words were hovering somewhere close-by in her mind, as ungraspable as a leaf blown away on the breeze. *Maybe it'll mean more in a minute,* she wondered, turning back to the letter.

Peterson explained that the crumbling of the ice caps had revealed something in the glacier which required further investigation. We flew for a couple of hours through the darkness and then lights appeared ahead in the sea and the sky. We landed on the ice. There were floodlights and white tents all around, and construction vehicles, bright yellow against the dark sky. At the centre of it all was a vast drill. We were met there by Dr LeoSirus herself. "We got here twenty-four hours ago," she told Peterson, without formalities, "and started drilling right away. The glacier is unstable." She led us to a creaking iron lift with a grill front and together we walked inside it, then lurched downwards, into the glacier itself.

"We expect the ice to hold for a number of weeks," Dr LeoSirus went on, as we plunged downwards, "but it could only be days. Maybe hours. We're at the mercy of the melt. You and your colleague will be fully sequestered by the military until your work here is done." As the lift screeched to a stop, Dr

LeoSirus dragged the grill open. We stepped into a corridor, lit by a few flickering oil lamps and lined with thick metal plates on all sides.

"We want to extract the items we have found down here as soon as possible," Dr LeoSirus went on, "But I wanted to take your advice before we get started, and I want your expertise every step of the way. Until we know exactly what we are dealing with."

We passed through a narrow, low passageway, hewn out of the white-blue ice, which was crackling with scratching, popping sounds; little messages from thousands of frozen years before. We were in the heart of the glacier.

We emerged into a large, circular chamber, where stood seventeen standing stones. Twice the height and three times the breath of person. Held in the glacier. Treasure locked inside for millions of years. A rough hole had been hacked into the centre-point of each standing stone, just below head height. I could see the very markings of the tools which had hewn that hole. And inside that hole was a rock: small enough to fit inside your fist, a rich, dark blue colour with a crystalline, grainy texture.

"You recognise the smaller rocks?" I remember Peterson asking.

"I wouldn't like to say at a glance," I replied. "But at a guess… carbonaceous meteorite."

"Exactly what I would have said," Peterson nodded, pale. "But how in the name of hell did they get down here?"

I had no answer. And no ideas.

We began. Extracting the first stone took several days, like removing the tooth of an unyielding giant. We needed new equipment and tools and tactics at every turn. Always under the threat of the glacier's collapse. At last, we had finally stowed the first great stone and its treasured rock above ground. We began our investigation into the smaller rock there and then, and as so many rudimentary geological studies begin… with a small taste of the rock itself. Peterson went first. He licked the surface and then dragged a tooth across it. He looked at me with a strange expression. Confused. Distrustful. He made some notes, but a short while later excused himself, asking me to secure the rock in the safe. I held it up before the lamplight, seeing its thousands of sparkling edges and wells. I took a tentative lick. Then a tiny graze of tooth on the rock surface. A taste. It was dry and hot, the taste of an arid summer's day. Soft in texture, like gold, but grainy as fresh white sand. Feeling guilty, I put it away and went to bed that night feeling sick and exhausted. I suffered night terrors that made me sweat and vomit and shiver the whole night through. When I woke in the dark of the Arctic morning, feeling worse than the night before, I hurried to find Peterson and decided to report my experience. He was already dead.

"Who's there?"

Failure froze. The voice was soft and deep but cut through the night like a dart. Failure curled up tightly beneath the gargoyle and stayed stock still.

"I can see your feet," the voice came again. And now Failure recognised the familiar tone of Smith. She shoved the letter into her back pocket, crept out and climbed to her feet defiantly. He stood before her, a tall, broad silhouette in the moonlight.

"Breaking the rules on day one?" He asked.

"I needed some time on my own," Failure said. "So don't go and hurl a whirling dervish about this. Did you know they've got a Sylkie down there in one of their labs?"

"What's that got to do with you breaking the rules?"

"It's getting tested on, isn't it?" Failure asked him. "It was all… I dunno. It was a sad thing. Scared. You see one of them scared in London Under? It made me feel bad."

"We're all making sacrifices," Smith said, his expression temperate. "As awful as they may be. What else can we do?"

"Drown, I guess," Failure shrugged, looking past Smith at the rough sea beyond. "Why're you up here anyway?"

"Just needed some air," he sighed. "I never sleep well when we're stuck on this island. Lucky for you I wasn't someone else."

"What d'you mean 'stuck'?" Failure asked, eyeing the white shadow of the yacht that had brought her here, bobbing at anchor, out on the waves.

"The sea's too rough to cross for now," he replied. "Happens more and more often the last year or two. Atsiler's chomping at the bit to get back to the mainland. Anyway, you better get down while you can. And Failure... this is the last time I'm going to cover for you. Mess up again, and I'm handing you in."

Failure hurried back to the lift and leaned against the cool metal wall as it descended. *He never would*, it hushed, and Failure smiled.

CHAPTER TWENTY-FOUR

After a fitful night, a hot, blustery dawn rose over the island, and Failure met the unfamiliar sun with relief.

You have one day to work out how to get to that lighthouse, her guts had insisted all through the long night.

I'll find a way, Failure had assured them, over and over again. *There's always a way.*

Doctor Norwood came to collect Failure from the dorm before Drill and, after conducting several tests and muttering a great deal, removed the boot from Failure's ankle. She put the joint through all kinds of tests, and Failure found the pain to be gone, and the ankle to feel stronger than it had before.

"You're all fit for purpose," the doctor had told her at last, with a curious frown. "You heal like no one else I've ever examined. Have you always been like that?"

"I dunno," Failure had said quietly. "Just lucky, I guess."

"Fascinating," the doctor had mused. "Well, if you feel up to it, you might as well join the others for the rest of morning Drill."

Thick storm clouds were gathering in the wide blue sky above as Failure emerged onto the Drill yard, whilst the rest of the first year completed a circuit session. For the first time since their arrival, Failure saw Desi. Dressed in his sports uniform, chatting with the blonde-haired boy Pride and a knot of others. When he caught her staring, he grinned and then looked away. Failure looked away quickly, a swooping sensation in her stomach, wishing he hadn't seen her stare.

"Take a quick break," the Drill instructor called to the rosy cheeked students, "then we'll be running the gauntlet."

Failure headed over to where Ness was loitering at the edge of the pack.

"I wasn't expecting to chat to you so soon," he smiled his fox-like smile as she approached. "Your second day and you're already knocking at my door."

"You said you can get stuff," Failure said shortly. "But how do I know I can trust you? What if you go scabbing on me?"

"Hmmm," Ness frowned, licking his lips. "That's a risk for you, I suppose. I could swear on something, or tell you my track record in these matters, or something equally as inelegant. But in the end, one supposes it's going to come down to how much you want the thing you want, ain't it?"

"Ok so how about we agree this," Failure said. "If you blab about what we discuss, in any way, to anyone, I'll snap both your arms at the elbow."

"That sounds fair to me," Ness replied, regarding her with an indulgent smile. "So, what will it be?"

"I want the code for the Perimeter doors. Any will do. Do you have it?"

"Ahh," he nodded, with a flick of his long hair. "A classic. I don't have any of the codes, but presumably all you really want is to get beyond The Perimeter?"

"And back," Failure corrected. "All unseen. Tonight."

"Then there is a way. It ain't glamorous, my treasure, but it's possible."

"Good," Failure replied. "What is it?"

"Ah-ah-ah," Ness shook his head, blue eyes twinkling. "First of all, I want one of those delicious little secrets you're keeping in your head. I can see them in there. You've more secrets than freckles, and that's saying something."

"Alright," she nodded. "Ask me."

"What's the story behind those gorgeous green lips of yours?"

Failure reached a hand to her lips self-consciously. "It's a stain," she replied. "Left by seaweed."

"I've eaten plenty of seaweed in my time," Ness mused. "Never stained my lips."

"Depends on when you take it, and why," Failure went on. "There's this sickness where I'm from, we call it the Blight. It comes in the flood waters. If you get the Blight, your chances aren't good. So, we've come up with this treatment."

"What happens if you don't get the medicine?" Ness asked.

Failure sighed, feeling the breath come from some very deep place within her lungs. "You seen that Sylkie in those testing cages?" She asked.

"Nasty, stinking one?" Ness responded. "Golden black fur and fangs?"

"That's the one," Failure nodded. "They come from London Under. Well, I guess there could be loads more of them now, from anywhere that's going under."

Failure waited for a pair of girls using their break for a jog to pass them.

"They're us," Failure said shortly. "People who get the Blight. If it goes badly for them, they start to turn."

Ness stared back at her but said nothing.

"They're deadly," Failure went on, "and they feed on meat. They're strong. Quick. And they heal too fast. Impossibly fast. You can't really kill them; you can only run. So yeah, they're pretty goddam dangerous. So, there you go. I had the blight. But I didn't change."

"I'm grateful for the knowledge," Ness smiled.

"Now give me yours," Failure replied.

"I certainly will," Ness nodded. "But first, let me tell you another little secret I heard last night. About your man, Desi. If you like. Then you can be in my debt."

Failure faltered. Being in debt didn't sound like a brilliant idea on her second day at The Programme, but then she glanced across at where Desi was laughing boldly with his knot.

"Yeah ok," Failure replied. "I accept I'll be in debt. What is it?"

"Desi was a spy."

Failure stared up at Ness. Her heart began to sink, searching like a scavenger for its shattered armour. "But he said he ran away. In the laundry," she insisted. "He said his family were prisoners in the biodome, so he agreed to come back."

"His father is a Baron," Ness said quietly. "The LeoMontague family already lives in a biodome. The Programme flew Desi down to London Under. On a sea plane. When the Major contacted them about a possible new recruit. It was all meant to be very secret, which of course, meant I heard all about it. They just wanted to find out who you really were, so they planted him right there with you. You've been had, my lovely."

Failure looked across at Desi, who seemed to feel her eyes on him and glanced across. His cheeks split into dimples and his brown eyes flashed like fresh cracked conkers.

Desi saved us, Failure's guts cried. *And we saved him. Desi's vulture found us across the impossible sea. Desi is our friend. Our first and only friend. And something more. Isn't he? Desi can't be a spy.*

A swarm of sharp, bitter betrayal began to gather in Failure's guts like a plague of locusts. She looked away from him and fought back hot, stinging tears.

"Seems like you were thick as thieves," Ness said quietly, "and I thought you better know the truth. Because everyone else does."

The plague of locusts flew into Failure's ears and eyes and mouth, choking her with disgust and hatred and the most bitter, agonising disappointment. She let them inside, let them clog her blood, her throat, her pounding heart. The dimples in Desi's cheeks were endearing. His conker brown eyes were disarming. Desi was troubled and charming and beautiful, and it had all been part of the plan; a plan which she had swallowed whole, like a fish on a hook. She felt raw with shame and rage. The locust swarm made their way through the pit of her stomach and began driving up and circling her heart, cutting it with thousands of tiny wings.

Failure grabbed a large, rough black rock from the turf beside her. She could feel the skull in his head cracking beneath the weight of the old remnant of volcanic stone. She could imagine how his beautiful face would look under the kiss of that crushing. But the Drill master stepped right in the path of herself and Ness, barking, "Alright, everyone get lined up at the assault course, you're all going to run the gauntlet. I'll take you six at a time. Look lively."

Failure drove the black rock into the brown earth at her feet. She stared at the glistening crystal formations in the rock as hard as her eyes could stare, in case she fell apart into a pile of bloody bones on the grassy bank.

"I get it," she managed to say in a hushed voice to Ness. "It was a good idea. To investigate me before I got let in. So, they planted a spy. I'd probably have done the same."

"That's very sportsmanlike," Ness replied. "Now, before we have to run the course, let me tell you how to get around that pesky old Perimeter, eh."

CHAPTER TWENTY-FIVE

A shrill whistle sounded as the Drill instructor sent the first six pupils scrambling across the course. There was a rumble from the sky above and a very light, warm drizzle began to fall. No one ran for cover. The poison rain still had no eye on Eylan Morr.

Failure turned her face upwards and closed her eyes, letting the drizzle fall on her skin, cool and soft. She opened her mouth and, beyond the slight aftertaste of seaweed, she could taste the earthy nothingness of distant mountain paths and ancient glaciers.

"Morning Failure," said a voice beside her, making her jump and open her eyes. Desi smiled at her brilliantly, his dimpled cheeks flushed. The shadow of green still clung to his lips. The shadow of Kezia's wings flapped overhead. "How're you getting on at Eylan Morr?"

"You lied to me," she said, not bothering to lower her tone, as dozens of pairs of eyes turned to watch their exchange. "And I will never forget it. Don't talk to me like we're friends."

A hot wind blew across the arena, making the drizzling mist feel cooler and wetter. It tugged Failure's tangled, ashy hair loose of its bindings.

She felt vulnerable and stupid, raw and unkempt.

"What d'you mean?" he asked with an infuriating smile.

Though every fibre in her being longed to rip his eyes out and shove them down his throat, she replied, "I know all about you and Doom. That's what I mean."

"Look, there's nothing going on with me or any girl on this island," Desi frowned, and nearby someone laughed. "Let's not argue about stuff we can't change. I wanted to ask you something," he added, a grin still dancing on his features. "Every time there's a travelling there's a formal dance. That's the day after tomorrow. Well, everyone's allowed to take someone to the dance."

Failure's heart blossomed with longing. Her stomach writhed with delicious nerves.

Desi is a spy, her guts howled at her, appalled. *A scab.*

And yet, ached her heart. *And yet.*

"So, my friend Pride, he hasn't invited anyone yet, but he's a kind of popular guy." There were whistles and giggles from the crowd beyond, and Desi stepped closer to Failure, the closest he had been since leaving her room on the yacht. "The girls and guys I hang out with, we have this place we go, for a kind of after-party thing," he said in a quiet voice. "Off the record. We have some stuff to drink and eat and, you know… We think you'd be fun to party with. So, could Pride ask you?"

Failure held back hot tears and tingling fists. She wanted to make contact with his jaw and skull, to thrash and thump his beautiful face until the painful fire in her blood was out, then hold his face and mend the wounds with salt grit kisses. But this place was nothing like home; there would be trouble here if she ripped his eyes out.

"Bygones are bygones," Desi said. "Come and hang out with us."

"I hate you like I've never hated anyone," Failure seethed through gritted teeth, his face only inches from hers. "You are the worst person."

Desi scowled and stood tall. "That's pathetic. But fine, hate me, then," he called back at her in a jovial, careless tone, as he sauntered back to his knot through the watching crowd, "see how much good that does you in a place like this."

"Alright, Kingsly, LeoMontague, you're up next," shouted the Drill instructor. "Plus, you three there and… new girl, you're up. Take it easy if you're still rehabilitating."

Failure lined up at the foot of the cargo nets beside Desi and his friends.

You've got to beat him, her guts urged wrathfully, flooding her body with fire.

Goddam right, Failure scowled.

The instructor blew his whistle, and Failure hauled herself quickly and easily up the rough blue rope of the cargo net, taking an early lead. As she swung over the top bar and scrambled down the other side of the nets, Failure came face to face with Desi through the ropes, a jolting sensation in her stomach. She hit the ground on the other side in first place, but she lost ground in a weightlifting exercise which followed and set off for a maze of zig zagging balance beams in last place.

The leaders picked their way along the beams, above a shallow pool of muddy water. They were steady and strong thanks to years of gymnastics, muscle conditioning, endless drills. But Failure, untrained and without caution, hit the beams like an alley cat above the poisoned flood. The delighted crowd shouted and jeered as she caught the pack.

Failure drew nearer to Desi, her heart hammering, feet quick along the narrow beam. They drew neck and neck, glanced at one another before accelerating and then colliding. Failure reached out and shoved Desi with a thwack of a fist, but his greater weight meant that the strike only made him stumble, whilst the force of it sent her sailing sideways, off the beam, through the cold grey drizzle and landing hard with a splash, face down in the muddy water. Desi streaked away without a backward glance. There was laughter from the benches, and the Drill master came shouting and ranting through the rain. Failure sat up in the muddy bog, her ankle smarting. She was drenched. Filthy. Soaked.

Failure.

The word came to her in the water.

Failure.

The voice was raw and empty. It did not sound. It seeped inside her, through the rain. Then came a low growling. A whimpering. A scratching of claw on stone. Failure climbed to her feet, blinking in the rain. It came from behind the wall beside her. The rain streamed down the grey concrete in rivulets. She pressed her hand to the surface.

Help. Me.

A stab of terror and unbearable pain shot through her being. She wrenched her hand back and stumbled again into the pool of mud. On the other side of the wall, footsteps sounded. A key was turned in a lock and a cage door creaked open. The whimpering turned into howls, and plumes of hot, rancid breath rose on the other side of the wall into the gathering storm. The Sylkie cage was on the other side of this wall. And its inhabitant was being taken for live testing. The Drill master was calling to her as he approached at a run. "Fitznil, get inside, now. Straight to the Headmaster's office."

CHAPTER TWENTY-SIX

Headmaster Isherwood sat on the far side of a large desk, wearing an ice-cold glare, a tweed suit and a taxidermy snake around his neck. The office was large, with one glass wall overlooking the plateau beyond.

"Good morning, Failure," Isherwood said in his quiet voice, once Failure had been shown inside. "Major Atsiler needs to have a word with you. I've been curious to meet you in person, so we thought we would kill all the birds with one stone, if you see what I mean."

"So, this isn't to do with the thing on the balance beams?" Failure asked, icy sweat breaking out on her palms and scalp as relief thrummed through her.

"What thing on the balance beams is that?" He asked, with an eyebrow raised.

"Oh, nothing. I fell off," she lied, glancing across at Major Atsiler, who sat on the near side of the desk, reclined in her chair.

"It's nice to see you looking well, Failure," she said. "That ankle healed fast."

"Yeah, its fine," Failure shrugged.

"Then let's have a little chat about your anchor."

"Still dunno jack-snap-shut about them," Failure replied.

"The Anchor is the tool that students use to hold them both in and through matter and time," Atsiler explained. "It is the hope we have of one day being able to bring travellers back. Each pupil is given the opportunity to select a single item which has some powerful significance to them. It becomes their anchor."

"Even a pet?" Failure asked, thinking of Kezia, swooping above her and Desi on the water.

"Animals make the strongest anchors," Atsiler replied. "But they carry the greatest risk. A student can only have one Anchor, Failure. If the animal itself were to come to harm, the student's chance at travelling would be obliterated. Only for the bold. Have you ever felt a sudden desire to grab at something you wanted? An item you just could not bear to part with? Whatever it may be. However humble or grand. Something you feel you would just despair if you had to be without?"

Failure felt the absence of the pocket watch at her breast. She longed for its familiar rhythm and frantic tick, the way it whispered to her, the echo of its precious ticking. "Yes," she breathed. "I know exactly what you're talking about."

"Indeed," Atsiler mused, a hunger sparking in her eye. "This is wonderful news, Failure. What is the item?"

"A Zeeva model twelve," Failure lied. "Serbian. Four-trigger system, detachable bolt magazine. Fully underwater compatible."

"I'm sorry..." Master Isherwood cut in. "I don't know what you're describing."

"The best goddam crossbow in the world," Failure grinned. She risked a glance at Atsiler, who's muscles tightened and teeth clenched.

"You mean... you want your Anchor to be... a weapon?" the Headmaster asked quietly.

Failure smiled and nodded. That was exactly what she wanted.

"I would be rather concerned about taking your Anchor request to the Governing Board for approval," Headmaster Isherwood mused, eyeing Failure.

"But there are loads of crossbows on the island," Failure said. "All the Governesses have them."

"Yes, Failure," Atsiler cut in, "But none of the children."

"I see," Failure said slowly. "The thing is, I can't change what I feel instinctively."

"No..." the Major mused, "but perhaps after some more reflection you will feel differently. It would make things very difficult for the staff, Failure, if a student was walking about with a weapon. And I'm sure the last thing you want to do is cause any trouble. Is it not? Perhaps you would like to hear about Smith's predicament, whilst we're here?"

"What predicament?" Failure asked.

"Doctor Norwood has concluded that Smith is unlikely to ever regain the use of his right arm," Atsiler told her, cooly. "The one that was injured on the yacht. When he saved your life."

"Is he gonna lose his job?" Failure asked quietly.

"Smith most certainly won't be following the career that he would have had," the Major replied. "Of course, I might have a place for him in my team. Long term. Smith is a promising officer. But I'd have to feel that it was all worth it."

"What d'you mean?" Failure questioned, as a small, sly smile crept over the Major's face.

"I'd want to feel that Smith's sacrifice had been worthwhile," Atsiler went on. "If I were to bring him into my permanent staff, I'd have to feel that your journey here at the Programme was going to be a success; that you would make good choices. For example, that you wouldn't dream of requesting to be armed with a crossbow for the duration of your studies here. Anchor or no anchor."

"Everyone's armed at home," Failure muttered. "I didn't think it would be such a big deal. If it means you'll keep Smith in your team, then I can just think of something else."

"I think that's an excellent idea," Major Atsiler beamed. "And Failure, please choose something which isn't a deadly threat to all of your colleagues and superiors, this time. I will trust you with this, even after I'm gone."

"You're leaving, then?" Failure asked.

"That's right," the Major smiled, glancing at the Headmaster. "The supply vessel should be arriving and departing whenever there's a break in the bad water. And so, our journey will continue."

"Well, that's not quite settled, then," said the Headmaster. "You may go and join your friends at lunch, Failure. It was very nice to meet you." Failure made her way to the door in silence.

In the corridor beyond, Dr Norwood was stood waiting patiently in her white coat, pale blonde hair tied back in its tight bun. She glanced at Failure as they passed one another, and a look flashed through the Doctor's pale brown eyes. Something Failure could not pin down. Nothing threatening nor or aggressive, but something that sent a chill down her spine. It was pity.

CHAPTER TWENTY-SEVEN

That night, as her roommates breathed rhythmically in their sleep, Failure slipped from her top bunk, past the sleeping Ness, and out into the deserted corridors.

Even if we make it, even if what Ness told you is right, what are you going to do when we get outside the Perimeter? her guts worried. *How will we find our way?*

It's a lighthouse, Failure replied. *You can see it for miles.*

Her heart thudded in the near silence. *Trouble. Ahead.*

She padded quietly through deserted corridors in her black trainers, heading for the outer quad. The first two doors she tried to exit through were locked, but the third opened with a sigh. She hurried in the shadows until she came to the courtyard lined with cages. The creatures shuffled nervously behind their bars as Failure headed, as Ness had instructed, to the metal grill in the centre of the quad. The rank, foul smell of Sylkie wafted towards her on the breeze. Ignoring it, Failure dropped to her knees at the grill and, after a quick glance to be sure she was alone, took it firmly in her hands. As Ness had promised, the grill came away with a few firm tugs, sending Failure sprawling on her backside. She looked down into the black tunnel with dread. It was dripping and damp, clogged with fur and dirt and the scent of decay.

This is a stupid idea, her guts replied in fury. *Do not go down there.*

But Failure lowered herself into the abyss headfirst, finding the tunnel to be only slightly wider than her shoulders. She dragged the grate back over and left it very slightly ajar, then began to inch through the sickening concrete hell. The smell was putrid, and the viscous matter she squelched through on elbows and hips made her heave. But at last, there was light ahead and the tunnel opened up, as Ness had promised, onto a grassy bank over a stream. Failure flopped into the cold water with relief, coughing and spitting out the smell of the tunnel, splashing clean water over her face and hands and forearms.

The night air of the beyond was light and breezy and warm. Keeping low, Failure crossed the tumbling grassland, heather and rock, until the lighthouse rose before her. It was extraordinarily tall and grand, like a companionless giant, stood waiting and watching the sea as it's white and red stripes peeled away with decades of neglect.

Failure grasped the brass handle and dragged open the front door. Before her curved a steep spiral staircase. She took the steps two at a time in the darkness. At the summit, she pushed open the door to the lantern room and skidded to a stop with an icy rush of dismay. The wind wailed through broken glass panes which lined the circular walls. The huge, ancient lamp in the centre winked in the moonlight. The black glass of the Time Programme buildings twinkled and flashed in the distant moon and starlight overheard. The roar of the ocean sounded on all sides.

Looking out over the island through the broken glass windows was the girl, Torment, who had picked a fight with Failure. And who hated her. It was a trap.

And yet, the petite girl with the short black hair only said, amiably, "I'm so glad you made it, Failure. Firstly, let me apologise."

Failure stared back at the steady, drawn face before her, ready to pounce.

"I'm sorry about the fight in the dorm," Torment went on. "I felt it was best to go in hard and create an apparent rivalry right from the start."

"I don't…" Failure faltered. "Are you here to fight me?"

"Definitely not," she smiled. "And even if I was, I wouldn't stand a chance."

"To get me in trouble for being out of bounds?"

"Again no," Torment replied. "How could I know you were here unless I was also here? No Failure, I'm here to invite you to join my knot."

"But…" Failure faltered, feeling numb with confusion. "But you hate me."

"That's exactly how it should seem," Torment nodded. "Let me start from the beginning—"

"I'm really not interested in your beginnings," Failure shook her head, her pulse racing. "Was it you who left me the note?"

"Of course," Torment nodded.

"Fine. Then if for some reason you have my watch, let's trade for it, quick and simple."

"We'll get to that," she replied. "But first, there is a great deal to explain."

"You talk like you've lived for a hundred years," Failure frowned. "Why're you sneaking around the island, leaving notes? And where's my goddam watch?"

"My name is Torment Joanne Bishop. I'm from Edinburgh. I was given a place at the Time Programme because of my unusual academic scores."

"You mean you're some kind of genius?" Failure asked.

"Some kind, yes," Torment replied, with a wry smile. "Shortly after I came to the Programme, I was offered private tutorials with Dr Alexis Mancini."

"What's a private tutorial?" Failure asked.

"One-to-one lessons with promising students," she replied. "Mancini was a researcher. Geology. She had a brilliant mind. And she was a brilliant engineer. After several months working with her, she started teaching me how to use a Galilei."

"Never heard of one," Failure shrugged.

"It's a time travel device," Tor explained. "Devilishly complicated to programme and manipulate. But brilliant, all the same."

"I thought the Programme's Travelling machine was called

The Conductor?" Failure asked, thinking of the great black glass insect dome on the plateau.

"It is," Tor nodded. "But the Galilei was Mancini's personal project. She believed that the Conductor was too aggressive. And she didn't believe that it would ever be able to bring kids back home. Her opinions on this were not welcomed. And so, she continued to work on the Galilei privately. She made two of them. One's on display in the Programme's Timepiece collection, here on the island."

"And the other?" Failure asked.

"It was stolen on the night of Mancini's death," Torment sighed. "A healthy woman in her early forties. Died one night, just like that. Strange, don't you think? But the robbery of a priceless timepiece and a mysterious death would be very bad for the Programme's reputation, so they kept it quiet. There's fierce competition between all of the Baron's to impress the Kala. Wouldn't look good on the billboards and news reels. The Galilei itself has never been found. Given that Mancini kept her notes encoded, most of the secrets of the Galilei died with her."

"Why did she write in code?" Failure asked.

"Because she considered travelling in time to be one of the most dangerous, reckless and ruinous things that could ever be undertaken," Torment replied. "She focussed all of her study on how to make it safe. And how to not make things worse."

"Sounds like basic common sense," Failure scoffed.

"Mancini believed that the scholars, engineers and teachers of the Programme knew that their own model, the Conductor, was flawed," Torment went on, regardless. "That they were unwilling or unable to change course, to admit failure and move forwards."

"Why would they be unwilling to do that?" Failure asked.

"The Conductor has taken countless funds to build. All the gold from the Claimings. Not to mention a decade's worth of utterly priceless time. So, they press on with their plan." Torment took a moment, chewing on her lips and staring off into the night.

At last she said, "We're guinea pigs, Failure. The remote location and the protection of the Kala means that the Programme can experiment with the Conductor without any scrutiny from the outside world. That makes us all very vulnerable."

Failure thought of the Sylkie, trapped and whimpering and dragged off to be experimented on. In the silence, Tor turned to look directly at Failure and held her gaze with a guarded expression, old before her years. "We can't leave the island. And even if we could, where would we go? Skin tattooed forever to make it clear who we are. I don't trust the Programme. Or the Time Corp."

"Good for you, I guess," Failure gave a shrug. "I don't really trust them either."

"The Time Corp and the Programmes are revered," Torment explained. "Mankind's only hope. Irreversibly linked to the Goddess. Even speaking against them in polite company would be seen as sabotage or worse, treason. By building on the research of Mancini, the team here can manage scraps of travel. Split seconds. But to really master travelling, they would need to use the Galilei itself."

"But they can't, because it's all in code?" Failure asked.

"Precisely. And no one's come anywhere close to breaking it. I doubt they're still even trying."

"Except you?" Failure responded.

"I'm not trying anymore either," Torment replied, a sly grin crossing her pointed face. "I broke the code months ago."

Failure stared at the girl before her. "Alright… she said slowly. So, what does that mean?"

"It means that I can go pastward," Torment replied. "No further than two hours back, at the moment. And every time I do, it takes its toll on my body for days. Yesterday, I travelled back to the headmaster's office and, unbeknown to them of course, stood behind the curtains during Desi's debrief. And this is why I desperately needed to speak with you. Failure, according to

Desi's report yesterday morning, you have been waltzing around London Under wearing a Galilei."

Failure closed her eyes and felt the moonlight against her eyelids, steady and strong.

We knew, her heart beat. *The watch. It was. Special.*

And now it's gone, her guts churned.

"After we came out of the lagoon," Failure sighed. "I lost it, when the Sylkie grabbed me. He picked it up. I knew he looked strange at the time. I knew it. And he betrayed me the minute he could. They're probably melting it down for gold as we speak."

"They absolutely won't be doing that," Torment replied, with her aged smile. "It's worth more than all the gold in the dying world. And if you join me, I can help you get it back. As I promised in my note."

Failure stared across at the girl before her, feeling as though the ground at her feet were shifting like sand.

"What d'you mean, 'join you'?" Failure asked.

"I want to form a knot with you," Torment explained. "Given my knowledge base and your natural gifts, we might be able to make it safe; Travelling. We might be able to create return journeys. We might save the whole drowning world."

But look, beat her heart, *where friends. Got you. Last time.*

"Please just take some time to consider everything I've told you tonight," Torment said, climbing to her feet and grabbing her crutches. "We need to get back before we're missed."

CHAPTER TWENTY-EIGHT

The air of the LatLong classroom was alive with a chorus of ticks, trips, flicks, shushes and bells. Dozens of glass display cases stood on the white marble floor, each filled with clocks, watches and timers. There was something beautiful and yet intrusive about the delicate, intricate whirring, ticking, spinning parts. Like seeing inside two dozen living bodies, their hearts and brains and bones laid bare.

At the far end of the room, the students were assembling around a display case where a short, balding man was calling for them to quieten down. His head was very round, with wisps of white hair combed across it. He was in his twilight years, and his green eyes were sharp and hooded by thick, unruly white brows.

"Alright, alright, settle down, we have a lot to cover," he told the class in a high-pitched Scots accent. "Today you'll be having a look at one of my favourites. John Harrison's H1 Marine Timekeeper. Flown up to Edinburgh by sea plane all the way from Greenwich Observatory Church, in the time of the Great Reformation."

Failure peered past shoulders and heads to look within the cabinet at the enormous clock, which was half as big as she was. She couldn't help but smile a guilty, wicked smile, remembering how the clock's old home in the Greenwich Observatory Church had been blown to smithereens by her own right-handed lob.

"It was later brought to the Programme by boat," the teacher went on, "which is most apt, as this machine was designed to conquer the ancient riddle of how to keep time at sea. You can begin by making a detailed drawing. Label anything you can, and we'll have a compare and contrast shortly. Papyrus and pencils are on the table."

Failure followed the crowd but the teacher intersected her, holding his hands behind his back in an old-fashioned, formal sort of way.

"Good morning," he said quietly, "and welcome to Eylan Morr. Here we are lucky enough to have, in my humble opinion, the most beautiful and finest collection of Timepieces of all the Programmes. You are a very lucky girl to be here, and to get to see them."

"Some kid was telling me about a Galilei," Failure replied.

"Ah yes, the Galilei," Master Godfrey mused, his hands behind his back. "A curious machine. Come and have a look." He led Failure to one of the smaller glass domes and gestured within. Laid on a blue velvet base, twinkling in the firefly glow, was a small, golden pocket watch. Several small dials were inlaid into its mother of pearl face, which was surrounded by a ring of bright rubies. Inscribed on the face in tiny golden letters, it read 'Fortiter ire retro'. It had no chain, but it was identical in every other way to Failure's own pocket watch.

"Designed to send the carrier on a journey through time and back," Master Godfrey was saying. "The maker was a member of the research team here at this very Programme. She died, most unexpectedly, about a year ago, and we lost all of her research along with her."

"The other one was stolen, right?" Failure asked, her heart thumping.

"On the night that she died," Godfrey nodded. He indicated an empty glass dome beside them, its blue velvet base still gleaming in the flickering lights. "I have always left the cabinet empty in the hope that one day it is safely returned."

"Shame it was nicked," Failure said, her throat thick, her heart thumping. "Was it exactly like this one?"

"There were some key differences in the interior workings," Master Godfrey explained. "Nothing you would have known about from a glance."

"Probably worth a few quid," Failure said.

Master Godfrey chuckled and began to shepherd her away. "Yes, a few quid indeed," he said. "But now, my dear, you have sketches to make and this is not a lesson on the Galilei but the Harrison; get along and fetch your pencil and papyrus."

Torment was right, her guts insisted. *Our watch really was a Galilei. They're too similar for it to be a coincidence, aren't they?*

I guess the stolen one was traded all the way down to London Under on the black market, Failure thought back.

But why in the name of the Goddess would Jada build it into a bomb? her guts demanded. *Unless she had no idea what it was? Seems unlikely, given what she must have paid for it.*

Yeah, I don't understand, Failure thought back. *And there's only one person I can ask.*

The morning dragged on until at last they broke for lunch, and Failure found Torment sat by herself in the canteen.

"What're you doing coming over here in front of everyone?" she hissed angrily.

"Desi was right, my watch was definitely a Galilei," Failure told her urgently.

"Keep your voice down," Torment snapped.

"Look at that, a couple of misfits having a little date," a girl shouted across from where she sat beside Doom. "Asking the new girl to the dance, are you, Tor?"

"You're gonna have to punch me," Tor hissed to Failure. "Or they'll think we're friends. I could punch you if you prefer?"

But at that moment, a knot of boys entered the canteen, making a lot of noise and distracting the crowd.

"Here comes your date for the dance, hey, Doom?" Called the tall, blonde-haired boy Pride, slinging an arm around Desi's shoulder.

"Who says I'm gonna forgive him?" Doom called back.

"Don't leave my boy waiting forever," Pride laughed. "He might die of a broken heart and not be able to dance."

"Well, we don't want that," Doom called back. "But whatever Desi LeoMontague prefers is irrelevant to me. I'm not planning on going to the dance. I want to be the chosen Traveller. And I want to make it. I won't even be in this reality anymore, when you're all prancing about on a dancefloor. I've never been fitter. Faster. I'm asking for extra work in almost every class, taking private tutorials. I don't see why I shouldn't be chosen. Goddess knows I've worked hard enough. Sacrificed enough."

"Just don't sacrifice my boy," Pride called to her. "He's mooning about with a broken heart."

"Why doesn't he just ask the new girl?" Doom shot back, with fire in her eyes. "Apparently, they got on just swell."

"She's not his type," Pride called back, "But you already know that Doom Van DeLey. He likes them high born and savage in the—" Before Pride could finish his sentence, Desi, laughing heartily, shoved his friend, sending him sprawling, clown-like, onto the canteen floor.

It's incredibly unhealthy to be jealous of a boy who you despise, Failure's guts told her angrily, watching Desi grinning as he pulled his friend back to his feet.

I know, I know, her heart replied.

"I need to speak to you about something else as well," Failure whispered to Tor as she got to her feet, invisible to the delighted crowd's cat calling. "Something strange happened to me."

"You're like a trouble magnet," Tor said, her lined face creasing into a brief smile.

"I had a meeting with the Headteacher," Failure went on, "and right at the end I passed Doctor Norwood as I was going in. I don't know why, but the way she looked at me gave me a bad feeling. A really bad feeling. I need to know what was said." Failure leaned in toward Tor. "I know my own guts, and I know something bad was happening. Really bad. I knew it from her face. You have to believe me. You need to Travel us back to that room."

Tor thought for a moment, biting her lip with her teeth.

"We can try," she nodded, "but it'll have to be in the lighthouse. Do you have a reliable way of getting out onto the island beyond now?"

"Yeah, I just—"

"Better if I don't know," Tor cut in, holding up a palm. "Just be there. Tonight."

CHAPTER TWENTY-NINE

That evening, the dorm was bright and busy with bodies and chatter. Ness's knot sprawled around the lower half of Failure's bunk, laughing, eating and drinking. Wishing away the time before she headed once again to the lighthouse, Failure was desperate for fresh air and solitude, so made her way to the Drill arena.

Almost before the warm night air had touched her skin, Failure heard the cry of the vulture. Kezia swooped through the star-lit sky and landed lightly on a rail close to Failure, her white plumage brilliant in the moonlight, her beady black eyes piercing against her bright yellow face. She hopped closer. Failure held out a hand to her, touching the white feathers on her back, softer than the finest silk. Kezia hopped onto Failure's forearm and nibbled at her sleeve. The door Failure had entered the Drill yard through swung shut behind her with a resounding click. The sound reverberated around the arena as though played through a microphone. Startled, Failure looked up and caught sight of a couple sat on the nearby benches, their arms around one another. At the sound of the door closing, they sprang apart. The beautiful cat-like eyes of Doom Van DeLey and the conker brown eyes of Desi shot across the arena at Failure and fixed her like bolts. Failure pushed Kezia away from her arm and stumbled back into the shadows, fumbling with the door handle, hurrying inside and dashing through the nearby, unfamiliar corridors.

I wish we could grow an armour plate across our brain and heart, Failure told her guts. *Get strong enough to go and bathe in the Thames Broad. Drink so much of its poisoned waters that we get the worst water blight you can, and change into something horrific, then swim all the way here and hunt Desi down and rip him to pieces.*

You'd never do it, her guts retorted. *You said as much yourself. You could never hurt that boy.*

Failure turned into a long corridor and took shelter in a small nook full of lab coats hanging on hooks and boxes full of plastic goggles. She leaned back against the wall.

He's probably telling Doom all about you as we think, her guts told her.

Didn't look like they were doing a lot of talking, Failure replied.

They can do whatever they like, they're nothing to us, her guts insisted.

Liar, chipped in the heart. *You want. Him more.*

Don't be so ridiculous, Failure sniped back. *That's completely ridiculous.*

I'm still. Learning, her heart beat back, somewhat unhelpfully.

Failure ran her hands through her mane of long, tangled fair hair and rubbed her face clear of it all. And then Desi was suddenly there, stood before her in his grey t-shirt, skin alive with triumphs.

"Why're you following me?" Failure asked angrily, making to walk past him. He blocked her way.

"I could ask you the same thing," he hissed.

"You think I want to be around with you and your lovebird?" Failure sniped. "I had no idea you were out there. Get out of my way."

"You've got to answer me first," Desi told her, a bright flush appearing on his cheeks.

"I don't have to do anything for you," Failure exclaimed, a fury boiling within her. "Who the Goddess d'you think you are? Mighty son of a Baron? Star pupil? You're a goddam scab. A spy."

Desi went to speak, but caught himself just for a moment, as her words seemed to register. Failure glared at him.

"Yeah, well," he replied, his face full of disdain, "we all get assignments. And anyway, I told you not to trust anyone at the Programme."

"And I told you to get out of my way," Failure hissed. "I might be late for something. I would look up the time on my pocket watch, but it was taken from me. Strange, as it's something private I was keeping hidden. I guess someone must have told them about that too."

"I've seen you speaking with Darkness," Desi seethed. "And I know what that kid does."

"Ness is my bunkmate," Failure spat back, "and I can talk with anyone I want."

"You're planning something. I know you, Failure, and it's written all over your face," Desi replied. "I should turn you in and get you thrown out of this place."

"Please go ahead and get it over with," Failure replied. "At least then they can just stretch my neck and I won't have to spend a lifetime regretting wasting my time on a scab like you."

"Just tell me the truth," Desi whispered, inching closer again. "About Kezia. I asked you before, and just now I saw her come to you again. Why does she come to you? Why? I want the goddam truth." Desi grabbed Failure's upper arms and she threw him off, shoving him in the chest and sending him stumbling backwards.

"The goddam truth?" Failure asked and felt a smile inching its way into her being. It spread like warm honey through her veins and coursed across her skin. "You want to know why Kezia comes to me? I didn't really know it myself. Not until right now. But it's because of you, isn't it? Because of what you feel for me. And she somehow knows it. I think you've known it since London Under. Hair like a village witch. Filthy nails. Green-tinged lips. It doesn't even make sense. But from the looks of things, I'm driving you mad."

Desi's expression hardened, and for a dangerous moment Failure thought he was going to attack her. But instead, his hands went to her face and her throat, and he was kissing her, and clinging to her, as though she were the last stretch of land in the drowning world.

But as her guts came to their senses, she pushed him away with a violent shove. They glared at one another, shocked.

"Stay away from me," he told her on ragged breath. The door to the long corridor squeaked as a knot of students came wandering by. Desi took one more look at Failure, then cleared his throat and, stepping out into the corridor, crossed paths with the students, giving them a casual, cheerful hello before disappearing through the closing door.

CHAPTER THIRTY

Are we telling Tor about the thing in the corridor? Failure's guts asked her later that night as they were dragged along the long, stinking tunnel which led to the beyond.

Nothing happened, Failure replied. *And no.*

I just wondered… would it make us feel… you know…?

Better. Pitched in her heartbeat, elevated with the effort of the crawl.

I don't know about you, but I'm feeling fine, Failure replied, driving herself onwards. *Let's just get there.*

The solitary figure of the lighthouse loomed tall in the moonlight. Failure hurried up the spiral staircase and found Tor at the summit, waiting for her.

"Tonight, we go back to investigate this Dr Norwood situation," Tor began immediately, without niceties. "And then I might need your help afterwards," she added. "It'll take me a while to recover physically before I can get back to the Programme."

"Ok by me," Failure agreed.

"Then let's not waste any time," Tor said, holding out her hands to Failure, palms up. "You want to go on a wild ride?"

Wild rides do absolutely not sound like a good idea, Failure's guts piped up with heat.

I want. To go, her heart replied, and Failure's feet led her across the room to where Tor was waiting.

"Give me the exact time and location of this incident with the doctor," Tor demanded, unpinning a bronze medal from her t-shirt. "This is my Anchor; my aunt's conscription medal," she explained. "We're going pastwards. I can keep us there for a couple of minutes, no more. I'm going to take us directly behind the curtains against the edge of that huge glass wall in the Head's office. Don't make a sound or move a muscle. As long as you don't, they'll never know we were there."

"What happens if they catch us?"

Tor frowned deeply. "Just don't let that happen. You're certain this is worth the risk?"

You must. You must. You must, thundered Failure's heart.

"Something frightened me," Failure told Tor. "I think it's worth the risk. I'll stand still and keep my mouth shut."

At last, the girl has a good plan, her guts chipped in.

"Alright then," Tor nodded. "Just hold on to my hands and relax your mind. I'm the traveller, you're just a passenger."

Failure nodded. Tor closed her eyes. A salty breeze sliced through the air between them, stirring Tor's short black hair and Failure's mane of ash blonde tangles. Tor's hands became cold in Failure's touch. Then came a tingling sensation, like pins and needles.

A chill flushed through Failure's neck and down her spine and she squeezed her eyes shut against the awful rush. A pressure began to grow in the sockets behind her eyes. Cold, shooting pains began to rip through Failure's shins, wrists and the back of the neck.

Flooded with a fear, Failure gripped Tor's hands more tightly. The pressure in her head grew until, opening her eyes, the world burst into an explosion of coloured lights. A twisting, shifting blur of colour swirled around Failure and Tor, sparks flying like a firestorm. As Failure gaped and peered at the mass of matter and energy embracing them, the lights began to slow their dance. And then they began to seep within Failure's skin, ice cold, like spirits of the dead, sinking into the depths of her.

Failure held on tightly to Tor's hands and squeezed her eyes shut against the bizarre reality into which she had plunged. The pressure began to recede. The air became hot and heavy.

Failure opened her eyes. She was stood in a narrow channel between a grey velvet curtain and a glass wall which overlooked the plateau. Tor stood before her, still holding her hands.

"You may go and join your friends at lunch, Failure," said the voice of the Headmaster, muffled by the wall of curtain between him and the hidden girls. "It was very nice to meet you."

Footsteps sounded. A door was opened. Now more footsteps came and a door was closed.

"Please, have a seat, Dr Norwood," the Headteacher went on. "And thank you for coming."

"What did you make of her?" asked the voice of Major Atsiler.

"Intriguing," mused the Headmaster. "Possibly trouble."

"And plenty of it," Major Atsiler went on.

"But we've had difficult students in the past," replied the smiling, light voice. "She will be trained and disciplined, and she will learn. What about the Galilei?"

"I don't for a moment believe she knew what it really was," Atsiler's voice replied. "But she knew it was gold, beyond a shadow of a doubt. That was why she had hidden it. She is a natural liar and sneak. And the problem is that you won't be able to break her. She doesn't understand even the concept of a rule."

"But she is young," Isherwood replied. "They learn at an exceptional rate. Supple, clear brains. That is the entire reason that the Time Programme system switched to using children as Travellers in the first place. She will learn, and grow, and obey."

"She will never recognise your authority," Major Atsiler said, adding, "I don't blame you for trying, Isherwood. What other choice do you have? And I'm not trying to encourage you to get rid of her. I'm only warning you of what I know to be true and giving you the chance to put in special measures ahead of time."

"What sort of measures?" Isherwood asked.

"Permanent, full-time supervision." The Major said frankly.

"We are on an Island, Dyani," Isherwood said, "miles offshore. In waters teeming with wildlife. I presume the girl can't fly? You say that Despair LeoMontague described the girl herself as being ignorant of her own power?"

"Entirely."

"And in your personal opinion, how much does the girl know?" Isherwood asked.

"I think Despair is right," replied the voice of Major Atsiler. "In my opinion she knows little to nothing of her gift. And if she did realise the truth, she would have no comprehension of how rare and extraordinary it is. I might be wrong. She may be lying or afraid or unwilling to share or demonstrate her abilities; a mistrust of authority is only natural for a young person who has been raised as she has and then there are the other fears that might keep her quiet – being different or fearing her own strength. But I didn't feel that in her. If anything, she isn't afraid enough."

Master Isherwood laughed a quiet, closed lip laugh at this and said, "I rather like her sass."

"You won't be saying that if she crosses you, Isherwood," the Major said cooly.

There was a long pause.

"I have heard rumours of the Gift, of course," mused the Headmaster. "But in all the years that I have been the Headmaster of this Programme I have never seen a spark of natural talent that could manipulate time in such a way as reports suggest this girl can; even Dr Mancini could not bend time by sheer will alone. The possibilities are incredible. They are terrifying. And they are unknown. My guardianship of this girl is perhaps the most vital moment in the history of this school, and in any of our lives. Failure may be the key to unlocking the very gates to Time itself. She must not know. The longer she can be kept ignorant of her own gifts, the easier things will go for us. Doctor Norwood," the Headteacher went on, "I'm keen to hear your findings, if you will."

"Yes, Sir," said the voice of the young Doctor. "Failure is now what we would consider fit and well. Her ankle is repaired and strong. The injury she sustained from the electric current of the eel has had no lasting effects. She is perfect."

"Very good," the Headmaster replied. "Very good."

"I don't know if I'm making myself plain, Sir," the Doctor went on, and now her voice became querulous. "Failure is perfect. Her wounds just… heal. Unnaturally fast. That ankle, when I set and bound it, had been broken. She can already run on it like an athlete. If the story of the electric eel is true, which I would be otherwise inclined to question, the injury might well have killed her. Instead of which, Officer Smith reports that within half an hour of finding her unconscious, she was firing a crossbow and racing across London Under."

"What does it mean for us?" the Headmaster purred.

There was a short pause. Failure and Tor stared at one another in the heavy silence. Tor's brow was beginning to pearl with beads of sweat. They didn't have long.

"If you were looking for a person with whom you might explore the very limits of science itself," Doctor Norwood said, her voice tremulous, "then this may be the person you were looking for."

"And how will we know the limits of what we can subject her to?" the Headmaster's voice asked.

"There is only one way to know that in such unprecedented circumstances, Sir," the doctor replied. "And when we are under such urgent time pressures."

"And it is?"

"Trial and error," the Doctor replied. "And error, in this instance, is likely to prove fatal."

Failure saw her own expression of horror reflected in Tor's face. The girl's hands were clammy and she began to close her eyes in concentration. Whatever she was holding onto, it was slipping.

"Failure is a gift to us from the Goddess," the Headmaster said, his voice barely audible beyond the curtain. "She will not leave this island until we have explored and exploited her potential to its absolute end."

The world before Failure began to melt. The glass window overlooking the plateau, the heavy grey velvet curtain, Tor's image, all swooning into one dribbling mess, like an oil painting melting in a fire.

When she opened her eyes, Failure was stood in the cool, silver light of the lamp room, still holding hands with Tor. As Failure steadied herself, feeling a little sick, Tor took several staggering steps and then collapsed.

CHAPTER THIRTY-ONE

"You shouldn't have kept us there so long," Failure insisted, helping Tor to sit up.

"I'll be fine," Tor replied in a shuddering stutter. "You're the one in real danger."

"Yeah, I'm clearly in a goddam pit of snakes," Failure raged. "Those neverspeaks are planning on testing on me, using me as a disposable lab rat."

"How are you feeling?" Tor asked her. "Right now? You aren't… exhausted?"

"Well, I'm fine," Failure said, with a shrug. "I felt a bit sick as we got back, but it's gone now. I guess it just didn't… take it out of me like it has you."

"One day you'll know how extraordinary you are," Tor breathed, "and then you'll see yourself completely differently. You'll see yourself the way I see you. When you know that for yourself, you'll be able to use your gifts. And then you'll be… you'll become what you can be."

"And what's that?" Failure asked.

"Still Failure," Tor replied. "You'll just see her differently on the other side."

"How d'you know all this stuff?" Failure asked.

"I was raised by Goddess' and Gods," Tor replied. "But the kind who walk the earth. People who love. Are kind. Work hard. Give. Sacrifice. Everything I am, is them."

They sat in silence and the blinking of stars. Failure fought hard to pretend that there were no tears pricking in her eyes, and Tor politely ignored her.

"I kissed Desi again," Failure said at last into the stillness.

"I had a feeling you would," Tor sighed, her ghostly pale face breaking into a smile as she struggled to bring her breathing back to normal. The moonlight winked in the glass of the vast lamp. In the distance, the waves crashed on the rock.

"Why're you doing all this?" Failure asked.

"My parents are members of the resistance," Tor said at last. "That's the truth of me, I suppose. I wasn't trained from childhood to excel at the Programme, like the rest of these kids. I was trained to destroy it."

"I thought the resistance was wiped out years ago?" Failure asked. "Wasn't that the whole point of the Great Reformation?"

"Exactly. A society so secret it doesn't even exist anymore. But it does, Failure. And we're getting ready for the coming battle. Maybe one day you'll join us."

"I don't even know who I am on my own yet," Failure sighed.

"What d'you mean? Tor asked.

"The guy who brought me up was a lying rat," Failure explained. "But before he betrayed me, he gave me this letter from my mother. I think it explains stuff, but so far it's just left me more confused."

"Who was she?"

"Some scientist," Failure explained. "She went on this expedition to dig up a ring of standing stones found buried in the Arctic."

Pale and exhausted as it was, Tor's head snapped up. "The stones of Hadrovane?" she asked. Failure nodded.

"Failure, the stones of Hadrovane are right here on Eylan Morr. They were brought here a decade ago. After the Great Quake."

The girls stared at one another across the darkness. Failure reached into her pocket for the wallet. "I think I better read the rest."

"Will you read it out loud?" Tor asked. For a moment, Failure hesitated.

You have to trust someone, her heart pounded. With trembling hands, Failure opened the papyrus. "They had found the stones and removed them from the ice," Failure explained to Tor. "And she had licked the rock, grazed it with a tooth, for some weird rock-specialist reason. She got ill, and when she came round, her colleague was dead." Failure took a deep breath and began to read aloud.

> Following Peterson's death the night before, the small carbonaceous rocks were being treated as highly toxic. Everyone assumed that I was Peterson's second in command, and so they kept me on in that position. I didn't argue. I was desperate to see what else we would find. I claimed I had never touched the things and kept my own reaction to tasting the rock quiet, fobbing it off as nothing more than morning sickness.

Tor interrupted, "Your mother was pregnant, at the time of these events?"

"Yes, with me, actually," Failure replied. "Why?"

"Just thinking," Tor mused. "Carry on."

Failure continued to read.

> Time was running out, small quakes were fracturing the ice more and more, day by day. There were seventeen stones, bearing their seventeen precious, toxic crystals in total. We had safely extracted fifteen of them at the time of the Great Quake. It came late at night. I was overseeing the loading of the fifteenth rock into a military helicopter at the time. The rumbling of the quake began. It was deeper and stronger than any of those which had come already. Dr LeoSirus came running at me, screaming for me to get in the helicopter immediately. We had to evacuate.

"Do you know who Dr Rosalie LeoSirus is?" Tor asked.

"The name rang a bell," Failure remembered. "Who is it?"

"At the time of your story, just a scientist. But Dr LeoSirus would go on to become the Kala. And she was working with your mother."

"None of this makes any sense," Failure frowned. "None at all."

"Why not?" Tor asked.

"I know a few other things about my mother. She was a drunk. An actress. A lover, not a fighter. Unhinged. Risky. Unstable. On the wrong side of the law. Living and dying in the bowel-end dive of London Under. Not this clever scientist. Not someone who worked for the Kala. It doesn't make sense."

Tor paused for a few moments, lost in thought, "Do you want to keep going?" She asked, and Failure nodded, returning to the papers.

One of the seventeen rocks was still trapped below in ice, the last of the sunken stone circle. We stood no chance of reclaiming it. But the sixteenth stone was lying on a metal trolley, a few metres away from the helicopter. The evacuation alarms started blaring across the glacier, and the helicopter blades were starting to spin into life, but I ran back to the sixteenth stone and ripped open the protective plastics around its heart. I snatched out the carbonaceous rock with my bare hands, shoving it in my pocket and racing back for the helicopter. I only just made it in time. If I hadn't, I would have drowned with every other soul. Instead, from the safety of the helicopter, we watched as the entire glacier, and the last of the secrets contained within it, fell into the water, shattering and thundering down to the bottom *of the sea.*

The world began falling apart after the great quake. There were seven more quakes that night alone. Flash flooding. Fires. The people were panicking. Looting. Fighting. I was locked away in Oxford with an armed guard and fifteen mysterious rocks and their fifteen precious, toxic *crystals.*

It became apparent immediately that the standing stones were rocks and nothing more nor less. But the small carbonaceous rocks which had been perched inside them on their heart shelves were something else. Unprecedented.

Their molecular structure was such that they could conduct matter. It was only days before we began experimenting with moving matter in time. Dr LeoSirus kept close to the research and instead of caution, or fear, she saw opportunity, hope and potential. The potential for time travel. The potential to save the drowning world. She was unafraid. She was inspired. She found backers in the military, and she hatched a plan. The royal family disappeared. Parliament was destroyed. And it all ended with a beautiful story about a Goddess rising from the waters. The cowardly escape from a glacier on a man-made helicopter was forgotten. Meanwhile, I began to experience night terrors, and then tiny losses of time, day and night. Whenever I attempted experiments with the crystals, the results differed to my colleague's work. I had consumed the rock, on that first night. It had become a part of me. I knew, or at least I theorised, what this would mean for my unborn child. And whilst I could keep my own secrets safe, I doubted that the child could have any control over itself, not whilst it was young. Besides, I had only had the briefest taste of the rock. My child had been growing within that contaminated environment for months. I had to keep you safe. I wanted to keep you, with a longing more agonising than pain, more frightening than death. But I knew that the only way to save you was to lose you. And so, I planned *a journey.*

My sister had already lost herself in Old London when she had deserted her conscription, and I had never heard from her since. But I searched, and eventually I found her and joined her there for the last weeks of my pregnancy. When I returned to Oxford with an empty belly and a broken heart, no one doubted the story that I told. That my child had not survived. So deep and brutal was my grief. But they saw my grief for the loss of you, not the death of you. You were safe. Never to be experimented on or exploited. Never to be used as a tool in a lie. Never to become a weapon in an unjust war. I had not left you in safe hands, I was sure of that. But at least you were free. I couldn't have wanted any m*ore for you.*

I write this to you now, shortly before I have to leave. When I return to Oxford, we are being shipped to an island named Eylan Morr, where I intend to continue my research, but am aware that my movements will be closely watched. Your aunt will pass this to you when you are eighteen. One day I hope we can meet and be together. Until then, be strong, be brave and be free. Whatever comes of your gifts, be they many, few or none, use them with your heart, and use *them kindly.*

I will love you forever.
Alexis. Your mum.

Failure held the precious pages in shaking hands. "The woman who was murdered in The Townhouse was not my mother," Failure said, her voice shaking. "She was my aunt. And Pa was her friend. Before he killed her. He must have read this letter. Maybe he stole it. Maybe she gave it to him. Either way, the goddam rat saw me as his ticket to fame and fortune. And he murdered my aunt to get his hands on me."

"Failure," Tor spoke in a voice full of wonder and fear. "I think your mother was Alexis Mancini. I think that your mother invented and built the Galilei."

"And that was why I knew it," Failure breathed. "And it knew me?"

"I don't know," Tor said with a dark frown. "But one thing I do know for sure, is that they will discover the truth, one day. And it will only make them more determined. We need to get you off this island."

CHAPTER THIRTY-TWO

Failure woke the next morning to Ness shaking the bunk. "Hey, Failure? Wake up, come on, get up!"

"What… what is it?" Failure mumbled, rubbing her eyes in the early morning light, which burst into the room as the curtains were ripped open from a dozen small windows.

"It's travelling day," Ness told her as he pinned up his long hair with a silver fox pin. "We have to get to the hall."

Failure waited for Tor to be dressed and together they hurried to the Main Hall amidst a throng of whispering students.

"A little bit exciting, isn't it?" Ness said, eyeing Failure and Tor as they entered the hall. "And this new little knot is all very cosy, meanwhile. Now I have a very important question. Very important question indeed."

"Go on," Failure said, with trepidation.

"What are going to wear?" Ness asked.

"I – what d'you mean?" Failure frowned.

"For the dance," he replied. "I just wondered… not trying to assume anything, but do you have something to wear? Because I have a spare, if you like? I wore it to the last dance but it'll look completely different on you. And no one would remember anyway."

"What d'you want in return?" Failure asked. "I'm already in your debt, aren't I?"

"Let's put that on the back burner," Ness shrugged.

"Why're you lending me the dress?" Failure asked, as Ness turned on the heel of his trainer with a smile and wandered away.

"I just feel kind of strongly about being able to wear what you like," he called back. "I'll leave it on your bunk."

"Hey, Ness," Failure called after him. "Thank you."

The headmaster emerged onto the stage. "Teachers, Governesses and Pupils," he began, as the last students grabbed seats and silence fell. "The time has come to announce the first student who will make their attempt at Travelling. Step forward, Mr Pride Hugo Kingsly." There was an explosion of shouting and punching and slapping and whooping. Pride strode to the front of the room, bounding up the stairs onto the stage like an award winner. He shook hands with the Headmaster, who motioned for quiet. Once again, a vivid fizz of anticipation gripped the hall.

"The second student who will make the attempt," said the Headmaster, "Will be; first year, Miss Doom Bernadette Van DeLey."

Joyful screams and cries of elation erupted around the hall, as Doom, holding her tiger cub close to her chest, got to her feet. She was beaming and being hugged and kissed by her friends like a messiah. Failure saw the fiery ambition in the girl's dark brown eyes and the determined set of her jaw. Holding her tiger cub against her cheek with one hand, Doom raised a forefinger to the air. Hundreds of students instantly mimicked her, sending their luck to the Kala. Doom walked down the aisle to thunderous applause and foot stamping. As she passed by Desi and his friends, Desi pushed his way out into the aisle and grabbed hold of her hand as though it were a dove. She slowed her pace, smiling adoringly and flushing red as he kissed the back of her hand. She pushed him away coyly and walked like a queen to the stage, shaking hands with the Headmaster.

"Pride and Doom," said the headmaster proudly, "you will commence your preparations immediately. I am sure I speak for every pupil at this esteemed Programme when I say that we very much hope *not* to see you here at the Report Assembly tomorrow." There was a chuckle of appreciation. "Bon voyage," the Headmaster finished with a flourish, and Doom and Pride were led away by Madame Zoya.

Immediately after the assembly were dismissed, Tor led Failure to the deserted entrance hall. In a shadowed corner, they came to a stop, staring up at the portraits on the wall.

"Firstly, you're going to want to see this," Tor told her. "Secondly, we're going to have to do something about it."

The portrait was neat and plain. A young woman stood beside a lab bench and stool, one hand resting on the bench surface, the other at her side, holding a silver compass. Her fine, long hair was the colour of the palest yellow sand. Her eyes were a serious, cool blue. Her pink lips were firm and straight. A scattering of dark freckles covered the bridge of her nose. It was like looking in a strange mirror at a fair, which could contort colour and shape, but not truth. A small silver plaque beneath the mirror read, "Dr Alexis Mancini. Geologist."

It's her, Failure's heart thudded, painfully.

It is, her guts replied.

"I didn't see it," Tor was saying, as a strange, hot, stinging sensation began at the back of Failure's throat. "She had short grey hair when I knew her. And your eyes are a different colour. And your lips, obviously. But when you strip all that back. It's like looking at the same person."

Failure headed for Drill and found the day to be bright, clear and scorching hot, the sky palest blue and empty of clouds. The students were just beginning their warm-up laps, whilst Atsiler's officers were packing up their things after their own morning regimes. Smith was pulling on a sweater, breathless.

"I need to speak to you," she told him quietly.

"Nice to see you too," Smith said with a smile. "And you'll be glad to know I've been made a permanent staff member with Atsiler's team. Why do I get the feeling that's got something to do with you?"

"I owed you," Failure shrugged, "But listen to me. This is actual life or death stuff."

Smith peered at her for a moment, before nodding and leading the way across the Drill yard.

They crossed the arena and Smith led her into the sports equipment store, closing the door behind them. It smelled of rubber balls and wet mud. "I've been wanting to talk to you, too," Smith said quietly, "and now's the only chance I'm going to have. You need to be careful around the LeoMontague boy. I know he's fun and charming and all the good things, but just be careful, ok. He's the son of a Baron and all these people are connected. Most of them are related. They're dangerous people, trust me. You can't... well, you can't trust him."

"I already know," Failure sighed deeply. "I know he was a spy. But that wasn't what I needed your help with."

"Well, whatever it is, you're gonna have to make it sharpish. The whole of Atsiler's cohort is packing up and getting off this island tonight. Life will be dull without you around," he smiled at her.

"Well, about that..." Failure said, a swooping sensation in her stomach. "The thing is, that's why I need your help. When you get to the other side. To the mainland."

"What kind of help?" He asked.

"I'm gonna need you to fish me out of a laundry bin. And set me free on the mainland."

CHAPTER THIRTY-THREE

Failure hurried to the deserted dorms to pack herself a bag with clothes and water, as Tor had instructed. Hanging from her bunk was the dress that Ness had promised her. It was made from delicate midnight blue silk, with a network of impossibly thin straps.

What's the point in trying it on? her guts demanded irritably as Failure stared at the blue silk. *It's not like you're ever going to get to wear it. We haven't got time for playing dressing up.*

I just wanted to know what it feels like, Failure replied. *To be one of those girls.*

Pointless, her guts moaned aggressively. *This is the sort of crud that your mother was known for. Look where it got her.*

She wasn't my mother, Failure replied.

As though climbing into another girl's skin, Failure undressed and stepped into the cold, soft fabric. She pulled the wispy straps over her pale, freckled shoulders.

She imagined another mirror. With an ornate gilt frame, dazzling in the light of three dozen firefly lamps and flickering candles on the top floor of The Townhouse. She smelled fragrant perfume of wood smoke and peony flowers. Scratchy jazz music played on a wind-up gramophone. The reflection in the mirror had the same pointed chin, large brown eyes, dark freckles and ash-white hair. But this hair was curled and tousled and sprayed with chemicals.

Beside her, a baby sat splashing in a tin bath. There were unshed tears in the young woman's eyes. She swayed to the scratchy music and laughed at the baby. She drank from a green champagne bottle with a gold label, holding it by the neck like a pirate. She poured the foamy bubbles into the baby's tub. The baby batted the bubbles delightedly and reached out for the woman.

She regretted opening the letter her sister had left behind, with strict instructions never to open it, but to give it to the child on her eighteenth winter solstice. She regretted reading the letter with Pa, in the rising dawn after a long night of revelry.

She looks across the room as the door creaks. She watches as Pa enters, holding a silver dagger in his hands.

"All the doors are locked," the woman says, her voice lyrical and sad. "And everyone's been sent away."

"You were always a smart girl," he says.

"But you won't hurt the baby. That's the whole point, isn't it? Because if I thought that, then I'd have to put up a fight, and things could get very messy for you. If Alexis ever finds out," she goes on, "she will kill you."

"I'll deserve it," Pa replies. The woman begins to laugh, throwing her head back, tossing the bottle of champagne aside, where it shatters on the floorboards. The record on the gramophone reaches its end. The needle runs over and over the last inch of record, making a beautiful tick-tick-tick-tick-tick.

"Doom are you in here?" His voice jolted Failure from her thoughts and Desi appeared on the threshold of the dorm, his face a picture of shock. "You aren't meant to be here," he said.

"Neither are you," Failure replied, her voice as cold as ice.

"I was… is Doom not in here?"

"No," Failure replied.

"Well. Sorry, then," he said. He turned to go but paused. He turned back, and there was a grin on his face that reminded Failure of salt sea spray drying on the skin.

"This is your 'look' for the dance?" Desi asked.

"None of your business," she snapped.

"It's just…" he grinned. "It's just so Failure."

"What's that mean?" she demanded furiously.

"You haven't even washed the mud off your hands, or brushed your hair," Desi told her. "It's the perfect formal dance look for you. And I love it."

"You know what else is so Failure?" she asked. "Is me kicking your shins off."

"Long live the Kala," he said, shaking a finger at the sky. And he was gone.

CHAPTER THIRTY-FOUR

After getting back into her uniform, Failure made her way to the assembly hall and watched with a sick feeling in her stomach as the doors were locked. It was time for the attempt at Travelling, and all other students were to be kept safe inside. Failure found Tor, and the two of them sat together, waiting in silence amidst the excited chatter of the crowd. At length, a low hum began to sound in the walls and the floorboards.

"This is it," Tor murmured as, from somewhere distant, an automated numerical countdown began. The humming sound crescendoed into an almighty bang, which shook the very floor, the glass chandelier and the velvet stage curtains like an earthquake. Then everything fell still, leaving Failure's ears ringing. A rush of whispered conversation broke out around the room, and shortly after, the deputy Headmistress Madame Zoya entered.

"Students," she announced. "Mr Pride Kingsly has made his first ever attempt at Travelling through time. On this occasion, he has been... unsuccessful."

The room seemed to deflate with an audible sigh and groan.

"The faculty are pleased with his efforts and will be granting him further opportunities in the future," Madame Zoya went on. "He is, as you might imagine, in need of recovery and rest. He is in the medical room now, and I will take two visitors to see him. Please organise this amongst yourselves and come forward presently.

"Meanwhile, Miss Doom Van DeLey has made her first ever attempt at Travelling through time. On this occasion, she has been..."

The fractious silence fizzed as a smile crept over Madame Zoya's painted face and she breathed, "Successful."

The room erupted into chaos. There were screams and whoops, whistles and laughter, students hugging each other and punching the air. Doom's knot were falling over to scream and sob and collapse in each other's arms. Desi, with Kezia perched on his shoulder, stood still amidst the wild joy of the crowd. He looked startled and sad and proud all at once.

This is a strange way to see him for the last time, her guts churned. *Seeing as we're getting off this island any time now.*

Madame Zoya raised a hand for quiet. "There will be a special report assembly held before morning lessons resume tomorrow. Tonight, however, enjoy the dance. A very good night to you all." Zoya exited through the dusky blue velvet curtain and the doors to the Main Hall were unlocked. Pupils streamed out towards their dorms to prepare for the dance, the name 'Doom' on all of their lips and reflected in all of their glowing expressions. Failure turned to Tor, her guts in knots of anticipation, and said, "I guess it's time. Let's go and check for any sign of the supply boat." At first, Tor made no reply. Her face was draining of all colour, to a deathly pallor.

"What's wrong?" Failure asked.

"I need to..." Tor stopped and swallowed. "Yes, let's check for the boat. Best place to see will be out on the plateau, by the main gates, you know where the white statues are?"

"Ok, let's go," Failure assented, climbing to her feet.

"I'll meet you there," Tor nodded, "I just need to collect something first. I might be a while. Go and scout out the laundry rooms for later, then meet me out on the plateau." Before Failure could protest, Tor had grabbed her crutches and headed out of the hall.

The laundry was hot with the tang of bleach and the pleasant, burnt flowery scent of fresh washing. As other students grabbed dresses and jackets wrapped in plastic from rails, Failure crossed to the laundry bins at the back of the room. They were plenty large enough to climb within, and full of mounds of sheets and towels to hide beneath. She would return later, when everyone else was busy at the dance and then wait to be wheeled out to the supply boat like a queen in a palanquin. And yet, a distant yearning tugged at her.

What now? her guts asked, churning within.

I don't know, Failure thought, leaving the laundry rooms and heading towards the plateau.

Gali. Lei. Her heart pounded, bitter with regret.

But there's nothing you can do about that, sighed her guts. *It's been handed over to the Headteacher long since. Even if we wanted to steal it back, we have no idea where it is.*

Failure's mind juddered like the cogs inside a faltering clock. She slowed to a standstill in the corridor, passed by students on their way to the Hall, dressed in sharp suits, elaborate, colourful gowns and glittering tiaras.

But that's not the only Galilei on this island, is it? she asked her guts. *There's its partner. Not identical to mine, but the next best thing in the entire world. And I know precisely where that partner is.*

You're a matter of hours from freedom and safety, her guts raged. *You have, for once in your life, a realistic and complete plan. The absolute last thing in the world that you should do right now is risk any of that, for anything or anyone, let alone for the old ticker. Absolutely not.*

But Failure had already set off.

"Where're you going?" called the armed Governess who was manning the main entrance, rising to her feet.

"Got to finish sketching the Harrison timepiece," Failure lied. "Master Godfrey said it was ok to finish up tonight."

"You want to work instead of party with all the other kids?" The Governess asked.

"Have you met those kids?" Failure responded wryly. The Governess smirked. "Go on, then."

Classroom 12 was alive with the flicks and thrills and clicks of its inhabitants. Failure passed between the display cases, which seemed to watch her as she walked, hissing *thief, thief, thief, thief, thief.*

The Galilei twinkled in its dome like a precious internal organ in a specimen jar. Failure placed her hands on the glass. It all just felt a little too easy. But she lifted the dome all the same. An ear-splitting shriek ripped through the room. So piecing and agonising was the sound that Failure herself screamed, covered her ears with her hands and in doing so dropped the glass dome. It shattered at her feet, spraying her with shards of glass.

Within seconds the room would be flooded with Governesses, and they would find her red handed. Failure acted in blind panic. First ripping the Galilei from its velvet base and shoving it into her pocket, she pushed as many glass display cases to the ground as she could, shattering them and sending their contents flying in a mess of cogs and bolts and springs. Finally, the sirens still wailing, she knelt amongst the shattered remains and, squeezing her eyes and lips tight shut, she smashed a carriage clock against her own right eye. Pain howled in her face and she felt hot blood trickle across her skin from her brow. Steeling herself, she smashed the clock against her lip and cried out as it split open. She was spitting blood onto a carpet of glass as the door to the room was ripped open and the first Governess appeared, crossbow raised.

"He hit me!" Failure screamed over the high-pitched wailing of the alarm. "He stole it and then he hit me!"

"Stay down!" the Governess shouted over the alarm's insistent howl, scanning the empty room. "Where did he go?"

"He... I think he ran through there!" Failure cried, pointing at the door to the back room. The Governess sprinted towards it, raised her bow and vanished inside. Failure ran.

Racing across the dark, deserted plateau, sirens blaring back in the compound, Failure saw the diminutive figure of Tor awaiting her beneath the white marble statues. Only when she was drawing close did Failure hear a familiar cry in the skies, high above, and glanced up to see Kezia swooping down and landing surely on the shoulder of her master.

"Why's she here?" Desi asked Tor as Failure skidded to a halt before them. He was dressed in a pair of black trousers and a white shirt, the sleeves rolled up to his elbows, Triumph tattoos gleaming in the moonlight. "And why're the alarms going off, Fitznil? Something to do with you and the bloody mess of your face?"

"I need to tell both of you something important," Tor explained quickly, "but time is against us. Unless you've done something that endangers us being here right now, Failure, it's of no interest to me."

"Nothing to do with me." Failure lied.

"Let's get it over with, then," Desi scoffed. "We're meant to report to the assembly hall if the alarms go off."

"Events have taken a bad turn and we're all going to have to trust one another and make some difficult choices," Tor said, in a shaky but resolute tone. "No matter what has gone on between the two of you up to this point, it has to be put aside."

"Sounds like a terrible idea," Failure retorted with scorn.

"It will be easier to show you than to tell you," Tor explained. "Which is why we're here."

We've got to head for the beach, soon, her guts warned. *Look, that's the supply boat out there on the horizon.*

"You remember Futility Watanabe's Travelling?" Tor asked Desi, who looked surprised and confused, but replied, "Of course. She was only about thirteen but she was crazy at Drill, and everything else. There wasn't a single kid who could beat her round the course. Youngest ever to Travel."

"That's right," Tor nodded. "Well, shortly before her Travelling I found a way to get through the Perimeter and started using the crypt of the old church as a place to work in secret."

"Didn't think you had it in you, Bishop," Desi cut in approvingly. "You're a dark horse."

"Yeah, it's the best thing about me," Tor replied. "Anyway, I was down there on the night of Futility's Travelling, when everyone else was at the dance. I heard people coming into the church above me, so I put out my candle and hid at the far end of the crypt."

"Who were they?" Desi asked.

"Half a dozen Governess' and Madame Zoya," Tor replied. "They carried something heavy down with them. A statue. It was smeared in some kind of soot or oil. I watched them carefully clean it up until it was gleaming white, then wrap it up in a tarpaulin. Left it there. When I was absolutely sure they had gone, I came out and took a closer look. It was a statue of Futility Watanabe."

Failure looked up at the white statue on the plinth beside her. The young girl was small but strong in stature. She was stood tall, raised up on her tiptoes, one arm held across her brow as though looking out into the distance, the other flung high, fingers outstretched, reaching for some unseen past.

"When the next supply boat came, months later," Tor went on, "there was a big charade made of unloading a brand new statue of Futility, carrying it up to the plateau in front of the entire school. Setting it on its plinth. Unveiling it from its tarpaulin. That was when I started to understand. That statue had not come ashore on that boat. It was already on the island. Had been on the island since the night of Futility's Travelling. Because it isn't a statue you see. None of them are. This is what the Conductor does to the body, when they overshoot the balance: Calcifies it; entombs it; turns it to stone. Futility Watanabe was the sixth kid of the Royal Scottish Programme to successfully Time Travel," Tor said finally. "Which means that, in fact, she was the sixth kid who died trying."

Failure peered up at the white bodies, contorted in the moonlight. There was a sharp, scratching pain in her chest. The stars in the wide sky seemed to lean down towards her. Six dead kids. Bodies paraded before the school like trophies. Failure tried to breathe in a lungful of cold air, but it tasted rank and felt poisonous on her tongue.

"You can see it so clearly, once you know," Tor was continuing. "Take another look. Futility isn't reaching for the skies or looking out to the horizon, yelling with pride and shouting with fervour. She's screaming. Trying to shield her eyes. Trying to stop the pain. Darkness Jones. Shame Sandu. Penitence Morton. Reckless O'Neill. Penitence McCleod. Futility Watanabe. All dead."

A tiny mewling and yelping sound came from the darkness beyond. A small, furry creature emerged from the shadows and approached Desi curiously. "What in the name of the goddess…" He crouched down and held out his hands. The tiger cub, Kimsha, ran to him gingerly and he lifted her carefully, taking the metal chain which dangled from her neck in his hands. "What's she doing out here on her own?"

And as Desi climbed to his feet, Kimsha in his arms, and the sirens blazed across the wide plateau, the implications of it all rained down on Failure. Sometime later that night another statue would be carried down into that crypt, in the cover of darkness. Another plinth would be erected. Another ceremony held as the statue was presented to the school. Failure closed her eyes and, in a moment of icy chill and shooting pain, imagined a beautiful, cold face, flesh turned into stone. She breathed in with a shudder, her breath hot, like smoke from a fire, and whispered, "Doom."

CHAPTER THIRTY-FIVE

The alarms fell silent across the plateau. Everything was heavy and close and hot.

"She's dead," Desi breathed, holding Kimsha tight and leaning heavily on the plinth at the foot of Futility's tomb.

"We need to get the hell away from this giant torture chamber," Failure said, starting to back away from Tor and Desi.

"Failure, wait," said Tor, her voice surprisingly soft as the white moonlight streamed over them. "She doesn't have to die. There's a small window of opportunity to save her. We can at least try. But I need you, Failure. Given the ease with which you move in time, I think you can do it. But all my current calculations run out at the waning of the full moon. And that's at about midnight tonight. After that, it's too late. We act now, or we can't even try."

"I don't want anything more to do with any of it," Failure replied. "I need to get out of here."

"You're her only hope," Tor cried, as Failure shook her head and turned away.

"I'm sorry."

"Failure please," Tor called after her. "Please think about what you're saying. You're going to let her die."

"She's already dead," Failure spat back on the rising wind, as the very lightest sprinkle of drizzle began to fall from the sky. On the distant beach, supply crates were being unloaded in panic; the crew wanted off the island and away from the treacherous rocks before the unexpected storm really hit and the waters became deadly. Supplies were scattered untidily all over the beach, crew hurrying this way and that. Atsiler and her team were amongst them, helping with the heavy loading. The chaos made for ideal cover. All Failure had to do now was get down onto that beach, grab a box of supplies and walk it onboard. Smith would help her with the rest. She was going to escape.

A mewling sounded at Failure's feet. Kimsha was rubbing her velvety ears on Failure's boots. She mewed again. Failure tried to ease her away with a gentle kick, but the cub took this as a sign of play and began snapping at Failure's laces merrily. Through the darkness, a figure approached, haunted by a white bird who circled above him. Desi had followed her.

"Can you please take the cat away?" Failure asked, picking Kimsha up and holding her out to him, peering through the driving, hot rain, which stole into her neck like tiny warm snakes. "And don't try and persuade me to go on this death sentence thrill ride through time, thanks. You're the last person on earth I'd do it for. And I don't even know how to do it. Tor thinks I'm something I'm not."

On the wind, or in the rain, a small voice sounded. Female and high and young.

"Kiiiiiiiimmm-shaaaaahhhh."

"Did you hear that?" Failure demanded, a chill tripping down her spine.

"What?" He asked, peering at her through the rain.

"Nothing," Failure snapped. But then, with a scramble and a slash of claw, Kimsha twisted in Failure's arms and bounded onto the turf, racing away into the night and the rain. She had heard Eylan Morr's ghosts and answered their deadly call.

"I know that I can't tell you what to do," Desi called to her through the deluge. "And I know you hate me, and her. But Doom shouldn't have died today. Tor says there's a slim chance of saving her. And that you are that chance."

"All the world's drowning," Failure called. "We're all going to die. All of us. None of it matters."

Holding her shivering arms against her body in the drumming power of the rain, Failure glanced at the easy route down to the beach across the slow-sloping turf of the cliff. The supply boat. Her ticket to freedom.

"I know you, Failure," Desi called. "You don't want me too, but I do. And if you really thought that Tor was wrong, or if you really weren't willing to try, then you'd already have run by now."

"Goddam you," Failure shouted at the boy with the bird. They stared at one another through the rain. From the shadows, Tor emerged and stood beside them.

"So, you're just gonna throw me back through time?" Failure called above the rain, feeling ashamed and furious all at once.

"Not throw you, exactly," Tor called with a frown. "I think it'll feel more like being crushed, if Mancini was right. You've felt it before, so you should know it when it comes. Although I think this will be… more. Can you both manage that?"

"Not a problem," Desi shrugged.

"What's he got to do with it?" Failure asked, looking at the boy through the rain.

"Desi's going with you as a passenger," Tor replied.

"Absolutely no goddam chance," Failure laughed. "I'm not going anywhere with that scab. Or any-when, for that matter."

"Well, you aren't going alone," Tor replied resolutely. "That's far too dangerous. Desi is stronger than me by far. He's the only one."

"He can't be trusted," Failure insisted.

"He's wants to save Doom. His only chance of doing that is to help you," Tor told her. "We aren't having any more discussions about it. Her time is already running out. Failure, you're going to need to choose an Anchor. And quickly."

"It's ok, I already have one," Failure replied. "Not on me, exactly. But somewhere on this island. And if that isn't good enough, I'll use this one." So saying, she took the stolen Galilei out of her pocket, sprinkling tiny shards of glass. Its gold and mother-of-pearl surfaces glinted in the flickering light, as though slowly coming to life.

"I nicked it," Failure said. "From classroom 12. That was why those alarms were blaring."

"You stole this from classroom Twelve?" Desi asked, his eyes wide as he stared at the priceless object and both he and Tor stepped closer toward her. "You are completely insane."

"They confiscated mine," Failure shrugged, "so I confiscated theirs."

"But there are only two Galilei's," Tor replied, her voice shaky.

"Yeah, I know," Failure replied. "My one, which the Headmaster has, and this one, which I nicked."

"I don't…" Tor mumbled for the words. "Wait. I need to think clearly."

"You don't need to get high and mighty about me stealing from the murderous lunatics, Tor," Failure went on. "They're what we describe in London Under as, 'fair game.'"

"But don't you see what this means?" Tor asked, pale in the moonlight. "No, of course you don't. You couldn't." Tor took a deep breath, pressing her palms together to steady herself. She looked up at Failure and Desi, a sudden, slightly manic, fervour in her eyes. "There were two Galilei's. Both made by Mancini, here on this island. On the night that she died, the original piece was taken by the faculty, researched and eventually displayed in classroom 12. It has sat there until tonight. The second one – the newer model – was stolen that night."

"Yeah, and it ended up in London Under and I got my hands on it," Failure explained to Desi. "As well you know, because it was you who saw it in the lagoon and told them, and they took it from me."

"But this is the impossible part," Tor cut in, as Desi went to protest.

"Why?" Failure asked. "A lot of that stuff makes its way to London Under on the black market."

"But the stolen Galilei wasn't sold on the black market," Tor said, her voice unusually hushed. "The stolen has Galilei never left this island." So saying, Tor reached into her pocket. From it, she drew out a long chain. At the end of the chain hung a golden pocket watch, with a mother-of-pearl face and a rim of ruby red stones.

"On the night that Mancini died, I had gone to her office for a tutorial. The Governess who had been stationed at her door told me the news, that Mancini had been taken to the infirmary with a suspected heart attack. That she wasn't likely to make it. The Governess let me inside Mancini's office to collect my notes. But I knew exactly where the Galilei's were kept. I grabbed my notes, grabbed the newest of the models and slipped it inside the notes. Walked away. That night I took it to the lighthouse. I strung it with this chain from an old pair of reading glasses, in case I ever needed to keep it close. Neither Galilei has ever left this island."

"So how the goddam did I get mine in London Under?" Failure asked. "There must be a third."

"Mancini only made two," Tor said. "Here. Have a better look at this one." She held up the chain from which the Galilei span and glinted, then rested it on her upturned palm. Failure reached out a hand and took the cool metal in her fingers.

Hello old friend, the pocket watch ticked its rapid, racing tick. *Here we are again.*

"It's impossible," Failure breathed. "My pocket watch is in the Headmaster's office. It can't exist in two places at once. This can't be mine. It can't be. But it is."

"Up until tonight both of the Galilei's have been on this island," Tor continued. "Until now. Failure, you aren't going to have to go back a few hours, after all. You're going to have to go back weeks."

"I'm… is that even possible?" Failure gaped.

"It must be," Tor replied, a winning smile on her heart-shaped face. "Because it's already happened. Do you see? It was us, all along. It's us who send the Galilei back in time tonight. It's us who deliver it to you, Failure. Albeit disguised in a bomb, which seems very… uh…"

184

"Very Failure," Desi finished.

"Well, yes," Tor shrugged, a dazed grin on her face. "Failure. The you in the past uses the Galilei to freeze time. She's selected for the Programme, she meets us and she ends up here, tonight. The only reason you are here at all, Failure, is because we have to try and save Doom, and in order to do that, the three of us send for you."

Failure stood with the thrill of possibility zinging through her skin. "But I don't know how to work a Galilei."

"You're the passenger, not the engine," Tor told her. "I'll do the rest. You just follow my instructions. And we already know what to do, because you've already lived it. You've already been back and taken the Galilei to yourself in the past. That Galilei in your hands passes from me to you tonight. You travel back and pass it to yourself. That Failure will bring it to the island. The Headmaster will confiscate it."

"It's all going to happen again," Failure said in awe, "the whole journey." She caught Desi's eye, and a feeling of something deliciously painful flashed through her. Kezia swooped down from above, Desi holding out a hand for her to land upon, but never taking his eyes from Failure.

"Failure, what was the date that you first came into possession of the Galilei?" Tor asked.

"It was… It was Samhain," she said, remembering the scorching hot winter day. "The first day in November."

"Only just within the month, to the day, thank the Goddess," Tor exclaimed. "That's as far as I know how to send you back."

"Of course it is," Desi said. "That's why you chose it. I mean, why you're about to choose it now. It's the furthest date you can get her back."

The three of them stood for a moment in the gravity of it all.

"The two of you are going to have to be very careful," Tor told them. "You mustn't be seen. You mustn't do anything to intervene or change the course of events. Doing so could be catastrophic for all of us and might result in you never getting back here at all."

"Except we have to save a girl who already died?" Failure asked wryly, causing an uncomfortable stir amongst them all. She handed her Galilei to Tor, who opened up the back cover and begin to set dials to precise coordinates. "We're about to end the goddam world, aren't we?" Failure sighed.

"It's already ending," Desi replied.

Tor handed both of the precious Galilei's to Failure, saying, "Use your Galilei with the chain to get you and Desi back, and leave it in the black box with the bomb. Then use the second to get you back to earlier this afternoon. Get Doom out of there however you can. Meet back at the lighthouse all four of us, and we'll figure out what to do from there."

Failure draped the chain of her own Galilei around her neck and slipped the other into her pocket.

"Hold hands," Tor instructed them both. "Close your eyes. Failure, concentrate on London Under and the day you got the watch."

Desi stroked the white feathers of Kezia's back and raised his fist to the sky. "Fly on," he told her in a quiet voice. "I'll back before you know it." She launched from his fist and flapped against the warm, wet air, and into the sky.

Failure and Desi reached their hands to one another through the rain.

"I have no idea what I'm doing," Failure replied, closing her eyes.

"Start focussing on that day now, Failure," Tor's voice came from across the plateau. "Bon voyage."

"What does bon voyage mean?" Failure asked, "Does it mean, 'go'?" But before Tor could reply, Failure's vision behind her closed lids began to twist and prick with tiny, white, bright lights. The world beneath her felt giddy and sickening. White hot pain shot into her wrists and shins and she gripped onto Desi's hands tightly as he gripped hers in shock and pain. As the pressure and the pain grew, Failure opened her mouth to exclaim that she was being crushed and opened her eyes at the same time. But her vision burst into an explosion of thousands of coloured lights, suspended in the air like sparkling shards of glass. The only other thing that existed in the swirling mass of colour and sparks was Desi, who held Failure's hands tightly and opened his eyes. They stared at one another as the swirling lights slowed and began to race towards them.

Failure and Desi grabbed for each other and ducked, sheltering their faces in the other's shoulders, but the coloured lights were upon them, sinking into their skin like ice-cold leeches. Failure fell to her knees, hiding from the icy lights beneath Desi's arms. A tremendous pressure crushed into her ribs and behind her eyes, along with a surge of intense nausea. At last, the pressure ebbed and then wished away, leaving her kneeling on the stone floor.

"Sorry guys," Failure said, beginning to emerge from where she had been cocooned in Desi's arms and against his chest. "I don't think it's gonna work." But she and Desi were no longer stood on the rainy plateau of Eylan Morr. They were kneeling on a wide city street which smelled of salt sea and whale oil. Before them stood a grand white mansion, and the sky was dark, gloomy and dull with black smog.

Through the gloom walked a man wearing khaki trousers, white vest and silver chain, his bald head shining with sweat in the sun. He was grumbling and laughing. A kid ran beside him, who he clipped around the ear, sending her stumbling. She wore jeans shorts, brown boots and a yellow mac, with a mop of long, tangled, dirty blonde hair. They had travelled pastward to the beginning.

CHAPTER THIRTY-SIX

"We actually made it," Desi gasped, his voice hoarse, hunched over and holding his chest. "I can't believe we actually made it. Are you ok?"

But Failure had already climbed to her feet and was scanning the streets, as nervous as a meercat by its burrow. "I'm ok, but… that was me and Pa, going by."

"It was definitely you," Desi agreed, clambering to his feet with some effort, dusting his arms and chest, as though to rid himself of the glassy coloured lights. "It was the other you, the friendlier one, from before."

"If you're gonna be like that then I'm leaving you in the past," Failure shot back, setting off across the street.

"Hey, wait, don't go charging off," Desi exclaimed, pulling her back into the shadows. "We need to think. Make a plan."

"There isn't time," Failure insisted. "That was me and Pa, heading back from the river. We'd been testing weapons, and we came back for lunch. Me – I mean the other me, the other Failure, she's going down into the kitchens right now to make something and bring it up to him. We have to get inside right now."

"Yeah, but you can't just wander in there," Desi said. "The other you literally just went inside. Let me do the talking. And hold my hand like you're with me."

Failure looked up at him, strange to see him again in the gloom of home.

"Fine," she said, "but if you mess it up, it's your girlfriend's neck on the line."

"She's not my girlfriend," Desi replied, taking Failure's hand and striding out across the street.

"Afternoon," Desi said cheerfully to the doorman. "You recognise me?"

The doorman peered at Desi with a look of distain and mistrust. "You're all glammed up like a Time Programme brat," he said. "But why'd one of them be in piss-hole-nowhere like here?"

"We're looking to set up a shop," Desi said. "Skin art. Time Corp replicas. Realistic, don't you think?"

"Kids and their fashions," the doorman smirked. "Looks like crud."

"Well, whatever your personal opinion, I need to get a private space to work in. Is your boss around?"

"Maybe," the doorman grunted. "You go up to the first floor and knock on the door with the brass handle."

"Thanks," Desi beamed, and they stepped within.

The Townhouse smelled of laced squid and chowder and fresh bread; of home and of childhood, which, Failure realised with a strange pang, had passed by. She led Desi up the broad staircase and, as they reached the door to Pa's office, dropped his hand from her own. "You stay here outside the door, ok?" She told him.

"Are you sure?" Desi asked.

Failure nodded and knocked three times. That familiar, scratched voice came from the other side of the door. "Who is it?"

"It's me," Failure called.

"It's open," Pa called back. With a last glance at Desi, Failure took the brass handle, twisted it, and opened the door.

Pa was sat on the velvet armchair by the window, fanning himself in the sweltering heat of the day. His pale blue eyes fixed upon her. In an instant, Failure saw herself through him; whoever this girl was, she wasn't his messy, chaotic little Failure, skipping and chattering at his side, full of the burning desire to please him, locked in a wall-less prison of loneliness, ignorance and neglect. Here was a girl in a Time Programme uniform, hair and skin soaked with rain that wasn't falling, her eye and lip bloody and swollen. She wasn't his anymore. And he saw it all in a heartbeat.

189

"Well blow my brains out," he breathed. "Why don't you shut the door behind yourselves."

Desi had stepped in alongside her. Failure glared at him in fury but turned back to Pa without a word. "We need to have a talk, m'love," she said.

"But you're downstairs making my lunch, kiddy," he replied. "So how can you be here with some grinning idiot pretty boy I never seen before? This some kind of Samhain prank?"

"It's not a prank," Failure said, crossing the room to the concealed weapons cabinet, masked by the false bookshelf. "But before I explain anything, I need to get some stuff."

She took out a handful of wires, fuses and dryweed-wrapped gunpower, placing them on the desk alongside Pa. He watched her with a mixture of curiosity and something a little like terror. "All I have to do is call out and a dozen of my people will be in here and on you, you know that."

"Yeah," said Failure, finding an all-too-familiar black cash box on a low shelf. "But I know you're smarter than that. And we have a lot to talk about." She selected a small, hand-held harpoon and loaded it with a couple of bolts. As an afterthought, Failure grabbed three of Pa's antique grenades, shoving them into her pockets.

"Put your hands up on your head, Pa," Failure said as she turned back to face him in his window seat. "I'm gonna tell you what to do, and you're gonna do it."

"And if you don't," Desi said, "then I hate to tell you this, Sir, but you're dead in a week. I've seen it. We're here to save your life."

A frown knitted on Pa's brow. "And how does it go?"

"I wouldn't like to tell you," Desi replied with an earnest frown. "It isn't… it's not a good death."

"You know Morningside Jack keeps dogs in his yard?" Failure chipped in. "They get hungry them dogs do, Pa."

"Morningside Jack hasn't been seen since the storms in last summer's whaling," Pa said, turning to her with a curl of his moist lip. "And you wouldn't shoot me."

"Don't test that," she replied coldly. "I need you alive."

"What've you done with my kid?" he asked, putting his hands behind his head, as though reclining in the hidden sun.

"I'll explain," she promised, "but while I do, I need you to make me a bomb."

"What kind of a bomb?"

"A good, big, helluva bomb," she grinned. "Impact blast. But make it look like it's on a timer with this watch. Desi, pass it to him." Keeping the crossbow raised, Failure gestured to Desi. He took the chain from around her neck, and once again Failure felt the wrench as her Galilei was removed from beside her heart.

I'll find you again, she vowed, silently.

You will, it ticked back. Desi laid it on the desk. Laughing, Pa crossed to sit behind it. "In you waltz like some nasty shadow of my kid and start with your demands. Why should I do anything for you?"

"Because I never asked you for anything else," Failure said, a lump swelling up in her throat. She felt tears spring to her eyes and wiped them away fiercely, but they sprang back again and betrayed her. All the unsaid things began to seep from her, the terrible wave of understanding hitting her like a mallet in the sternum. "Because I was a slave here. Because I know what you did. You knew I would be the most valuable possession you could ever possess. So, you killed my aunt and took me for your own. Hid me from school and other kids. You owe me so much more than this. But all I'm gonna ask you for right now is a helluva bomb."

"Alright, alright, just don't cry," Pa replied gruffly. "You're in charge, apparently," he licked his lips, then took the pocket watch and turned it over in his swollen red fingers and their silver rings. "What're you planning on blowing up?"

"None of your business," Failure replied. "But when the other me comes up here with your lunch in a few minutes time, you have to send her on a Task to go and fetch this little box from Mumma Dory's Chowder Cafe. Right away."

"I don't send my Fey on Tasks," Pa shook his head, pressing the block of gunpowder firmly into the black box.

"You have to send her on this one today," Failure told him, "and when she gets back from it, there's gonna be three Guzzers on her tail, and you're gonna have to hand her over to them."

Pa began to laugh his big, bark of a laugh. It was a dark thing. Desi shuffled on his feet. Failure gripped the crossbow more tightly and adjusted her sweaty trigger finger.

"Never in a million years," Pa replied. "Besides, Guzzers don't come into Fitzrovia."

"They will today," Failure told him, "and you'll hand her over. It's what you have to do. To make your amends."

"So, you come here in your Time Corp get-up, like some kind of time police, and tell me I do what you say or else I die?" Pa asked, licking his lips, sweat pricking out from his skin.

"That's how it goes," Failure replied.

"You're a brutal thing, aren't you?" Pa asked, closing over the lid on the black box bomb. "I see that now. I made you into a salt grit monster."

Failure shrugged. "You didn't make me."

He pushed the bomb towards her. "I've packed it in tight so it doesn't blow up in her face on the way. Your face I wouldn't be so bothered about."

"Don't worry," Failure said with a roughish grin. "We'll both look after it."

The faint ticking of the pocket watch bomb sounded between them on the desk.

"There's something else I need," Failure cut in. "You have to give her the letter. From her mother."

The colour drained from Pa's ruddy cheeks, until he was ash white. He stared at her, unmoving, a malevolent rage in his glare. "You got any idea what you're costing me?" he asked, his voice quiet, no hint of a smile left in his being.

"I've told you what you have to do," Failure said.

Pa reached across the desk for a bottle of pearly orange moonshine and took a long drink from the bottle, belching loudly as the poison took hold. "You can both go to the dogs."

"Mess this up and it isn't Failure who goes to the dogs, Sir," Desi said in a quiet, pitiful voice. "But let's not say any more about that."

"I raised her, you know," Pa said, glaring at Desi. With a twisted wince in her very soul, Failure saw that his pale blue eyes had misted up and were wobbling with unshed tears. "Whatever else I done, I raised that kid." He took another swig of moonshine, grimacing. "Sometimes, I even thought I might not sell her, after all. I sometimes thought I might keep her. Even set her free." His words were leaden in the poisoned berry-scented air. "So much goddam talking, talking, all the time, never shutting up. Dreamy about the world. Not like the rest of us. Just a tight little ball of fight and cheer. She's one of the only other human beings I've ever been able to stand."

"I know," Desi sighed, all the playful deceit stripped from his voice. "Me too."

Failure picked up the black box bomb and held it against her chest. The ticking resounded against her ribs.

"I can't believe you fall for some rich kid, Fey," Pa said, shaking his head. "But I do know that I don't wanna be eaten by dogs, so I'm gambling on doing as you say. Older, nastier Failure. I've made you your bomb. I'll do what you said. Now get the Goddess out of here." He swigged again at the moonshine.

"Don't drink all that before you have the chance to do what I told you," Failure warned him.

"I'll drink what I like, you little guttersnipe," he snapped back, halfway to darkness already. With a piercing splintering of glass, the bottle in Pa's hand exploded, spilling orange liqueur all over him. He screamed and glared up at where she had fired the bolt directly into the bottle. He burst into peels of raucous laughter. Failure crossed to the door. She looked back at him, where he was licking the pearly orange drops from the desk, glass and all.

"Desi, we have to go," Failure said. "Thanks for the good times, Pa. I should have escaped you years ago."

"And I should have sold you when you was still a baby splashing in a bathtub of champagne," he replied. "But who gives a goddam?"

CHAPTER THIRTY-SEVEN

"We have to give the bomb to Jada," Failure called as they raced from the Townhouse to Pa's private jetty, "We need to get to Whitechapel, and the best way to do that is on the water. Hiya, I'm taking a boat for the afternoon," Failure called cheerily to the watchman, and though he took a moment to recognise her, recognise her he did, and never got up from his seat.

The Thames Broad was growing just a little rough, in advance of the approaching storm. Salt spray clung to Failure's lips and lashes, her breaths of estuary air deep and toxic and welcoming.

"So how did you get the box in the first place?" Desi asked, "You said you nicked it?"

"It was just sitting on the counter out the back of the cafe," Failure explained. "But her lads came out chasing after me for it. They said it had to be back in the cafe by the evening cos Morningside Jack was coming for it. And if it wasn't back, they'd all be for it."

"Who is this Morningside Jack, then?" Desi asked.

"A kind of pirate," Failure replied. "Lived on his boats, mostly, a little fleet of them. Sinking and plundering traders, whalers, fishermen. Everyone's terrified of Jack. But he'd not been seen for a long time."

"But that has to be the story, then," Desi went on, rubbing his forehead with his hands. "If you don't start that story off then no one does. I have an idea."

"Good job, too," Failure said, as the docks at Royal London Hospital came into view. "We're almost there."

"Where do you find a kid with no money in this place?" Desi asked.

"Every street corner," Failure replied, handing him the bomb.

"That's the answer then," Desi said, and he led them towards a young boy with no shoes and missing teeth, sitting on the smoggy pavement a few doors down from the jetty.

"Morning, boy," Desi said in a cheery voice. "You want some cash?"

The boy nodded keenly.

"You know who I am?"

"No m'love," the kid replied. "But looks and sounds you a foreign type."

"I've been away in the sun on my boat," Desi told him. "As you can see from how sun kissed my skin is, yes?"

The boy nodded.

"Well, my name is Jack. They call me Morningside Jack around these parts."

The boy's eyes widened and his mouth fell open. "They said you was a dead'un," he gawped.

"Well, you can be the judge of that," Desi replied, "I'm back, see? And I need some help. Can you help me?"

The child nodded, his expression a picture of frozen terror.

"You take this precious box to Jada's Cafe in Whitechapel. You know the one?"

"Yes, Mr Jack," the boy replied.

"You go there now, fast as you can," Desi told him, "but careful as can be. Tell Jada that I want her to keep it for me till dusk and give her this as a sweetener." Desi handed the boy a twenty thousand quid note. "Tell her Jack's bringing ten times this much as a thank you by evening."

"I'll tell her," the boy breathed.

"And here's something for you as a thank you from old Jack," Desi grinned, handing the boy another twenty thousand pounds. His eyes lit bright and seemed to swim at the sight of so much money. He took the black box excitedly, made his repeated promises to old Jack, and scarpered.

"The other me will be arriving at the Cafe soon," Failure said as she and Desi sailed out into the very midpoint of the Thames Broad. She killed the motor and allowed the boat to drift on the natural ebb and flow of the waves. "I'm about to mess up the robbery and get chased all that way to that high hill over there in Greenwich." She pointed through the hazy heat of the air and Desi looked out over the horizon.

"It's strange to think that right now there's another me out there, too," he mused, quietly. "Sitting in Quantums. About to be summoned to the Head and given a secret mission. Flown to London Under on a seaplane. Meet a girl called Failure, get kidnapped, swim with water monsters, survive the blight. Kiss a beautiful girl and watch another one walk to her death."

For a long moment, Failure watched him through the river spray on her eyelashes. "You're a very annoying person," she said at last. "You're slippery and hard to trust. Like an eel."

"Yeah, well you've survived an eel before," he said, with a grin.

"I have, but it wasn't good for me," she replied. "You're so... it's so easy to want you. I think I'll always want you. But you lie too easily and too well. And you love it all. The thrill. You always will do. There isn't going to be a eureka moment when you change, and where you become true. Or constant. Because that isn't you. I'm kind of tired of wishing it was."

Desi watched her through the whipping wind of the open river. He smiled, his conker brown eyes so soft and so beguiling, the dimples appearing in his sun-kissed skin, his lips tinged green like her own, as though the kiss they had shared and would share again and again in this eternal loop, had lingered there.

"It's gone out for you, hasn't it?" he asked. "That spark that was there before."

"Not out, really," Failure replied, feeling the spicy hum in the air that meant the storm was brewing. "But I think it's getting dimmer the less lonely I feel. I sort of have friends, now, I think. Smith. Tor. Maybe Ness too."

"It's a shame," Desi said, looking out now over the smog-thickened city, oblivious to the oncoming storm. "I mean the spark going out, not you having friends," he added with a grin. "Friends are everything. Friends are better than sparks, in the end."

"Funny old world," Failure said, and they smiled at one another for the first time in weeks.

"I wouldn't go back and change it," Failure said after a while. "Our journey. Even if I could. Which I could, I suppose, what with the whole time-travel thing. But I still want to live through it all and come out on this side the way things are now. And go back and do it again. And come out of it again. I guess that somewhere in time we'll always be going on that journey together."

Failure breathed in the salt and oil and wished the city farewell. By the time she returned, one day in the distant future, she thought, this place would be gone.

After some time, there it was; a faraway explosion ripped through the peaceful skies, sending a flock of distant seagulls scattering up into the air above the summit of Greenwich Park. The Observatory Church had just been bombed. It had begun. Every ka-boom and capture and betrayal and hope and loss and theft. Everything that would bring them here. Failure took the second Galilei from her pocket and held it in the palm of her right hand.

"Let's hope Tor set that thing right," Desi said, moving to sit opposite Failure. They reached for one another's hands and Failure felt the mechanism whirr into position. She focussed her mind on her Anchor, back on the island. "Go," Failure whispered. But nothing happened. No crush, no sickness, no journey.

The Anchor isn't strong enough, she told her guts. *It's not gonna take me back. What would that mean? We'd be trapped here. I could wander down the riverbank and find me a little boat. Start a little fleet. Set up some kind of Townhouse of my own. Never have to leave home after all. Who wants to go back to being a prisoner on an island of kid killers anyway? Who wants to go back and save Doom Goddam Van DeLey?*

But her guts were unusually quiet. They made no reply.

What's wrong? She asked her heart, but it only beat a heady rhythm in response.

"Are you ok?" Desi asked, and Failure shuffled on the bench, clearing her throat and replying, "I'm fine. It just doesn't feel all that fantastic. I'm taking us back to the island of murderous genius' who want to experiment on me to save your beautiful girlfriend."

"You know why you're really going back," Desi said, moving closer towards her, holding her hands tightly, the Galilei closed in between their palms. "Same way I knew from the start why Kezia goes to you. Just look inside yourself and be as honest as you can."

Failure thought about Ness, offering her his dress for the dance. She thought about Smith, risking everything to spirit her away on the other side of the crossing. She thought about Tor, waiting nervously for her return in the lighthouse. These were her Anchors.

"Go," she whispered. A sudden, unbearable crushing sensation slammed into Failure and she fell forward, grabbing for Desi. Failure kept her eyes squeezed tight shut as the painful shards of colour began their icy journey within her skin. But the power of the Galilei was diminishing.

"I think the time's running out," Failure cried through the coloured lights.

"Is it not going to work?" Desi cried back, holding her hands more tightly.

"I don't think it's got enough power," Failure called, a pain coursing through her chest.

For a moment that seemed to last too long, Desi stared into Failure's eyes. In the reflection, she saw every freckle, the wild mane of her hair, the green of her lips. And then he gave a faint smile that sent a chill into her very guts.

"You'll make it, Failure," he called, "I know you will. Just get back to the lighthouse and save her. And save them all." He ripped his hands out of Failure's. The rainbow explosion slammed into her vision once more, knocking her onto her back, and senseless.

When she came to and opened her eyes, Failure found that Desi and the boat and her beloved river were gone. She was lying on a heather-strewn hillock, looking down over the black glass of the Time Programme compound. On the white path that crossed the plateau, four Governesses were carrying a stretcher bearing the moaning form of Pride Kingsly out of the Dome and towards the main buildings. Failure was a prisoner on the island once more. And Doom Van DeLey was about to die.

CHAPTER THIRTY-EIGHT

Failure scrambled her way down the rocky face of the hill and, with no time for caution, crossed the plateau at a run. As she reached the insect-hive dome, Failure peered in through the glass doors.

The cavernous interior was unpleasantly bright, lit by dozens of solar lamps. Technicians and engineers mingled with teachers and Governesses, the Headmaster and Madame Zoya, all of them wearing white lab coats and thick, protective metal tabards.

At the centre of the dome stood Conductor VI. It was a huge golden structure, reminiscent of a steam train. A golden throne was being carried to its centre, cables and wires draping out from it, trailing across to a huge control desk where engineers were hastily reprogramming a vast panel of dials and levers, an air of mild panic about them. Not a soul had an eye on the doorway, and so Failure simply stepped within.

Doom was stood at the foot of the Conductor, kissing and snuggling her tiger cub with great enthusiasm. "It's exciting to be the first traveller to use the new equipment," Doom was smiling brightly. "Even if it does look a bit like an electric chair. I wish this little terror could come with me," she held the cub up high, "but I'll be back for you baby Kimmy, yes I will!"

An orderly took the cub from Doom and carried it, mewling and pawing, to a cage on the other side of the control panel.

Failure crossed to one of the Governess' and said, "Hi, I'm meant to collect the Anchor and its cage."

"Shouldn't you be doing that after the attempt is complete?" The Governess asked, eyeing Failure's bruised, swollen face.

"Well, apparently the metal of the tiger's cage might be disrupting the attempt, like it just did for the boy," Failure said nonchalantly. "But I can leave it, if you want? I'm sure they won't blame you personally if it messes it up again."

"Come on and get it quickly then," the Governess said hurriedly. A golden crown was placed on Doom's curly black hair. Wires tumbled out of the headpiece, linking it up to the frame of the Conductor, and from there to the control panel, looking for all the world like an electric chair. Between them, Failure and the Governess hauled the heavy cage up off its table, the tiger cub mewling skittishly inside.

"What're you doing with Kimsha?" Called the sweet voice of Doom Van De Ley, struggling to see what was going on, as more sensors were being placed on various parts of her body. Failure tried to slip her thumb under the small metal catch which held the door of the cage shut.

"I want her here," Doom called out in a sudden panic, "She's my Anchor!! You can't move her out when I'm about to travel."

"Stay still!" barked one of the engineers, trying to keep the golden crown in place on Doom's silken hair, as she struggled against the wires.

"No, wait!" She shouted, panic and colour rising in her face, "What if I manage to travel but I don't know how to get back without her exact location? Wait!"

A scuffle began on the platform as Doom shook her head and dislodged the crown, and the two engineers fought to keep her still. Failure managed to get her thumb under the catch and flipped the door of the cage open. She twisted the cage. The Governess lost her grip. The cage toppled over, falling to the floor with a sickening clang, and in an instant the savvy cub bolted for freedom.

Pandemonium broke out. Doom began screaming in panic, fighting against the engineers, whilst Failure made a big show of trying to catch the little cub, pushing over chairs and equipment and engineers and Governesses, while the cub bolted for the glass doors.

Failure gritted her teeth and ran toward the same doors. She screwed her eyes shut and slammed into the glass with both hands outstretched. There was a shattering as the glass doors exploded under the sudden impact. Failure flew through the doorway in an arc of broken shards. With a streak of orange and black, Kimsha was gone. Doom Van DeLey had lost her Anchor. She could no longer travel. Failure had saved her.

The tight grip of a Governess's hand closed about Failure's upper arm. She was hauled to her feet and led hastily back inside the Dome and through to a large laboratory off the side of the main atrium.

The sobbing form of Doom Van DeLey was brought inside and a Governess helped her to sit down on a lab stool, handing her a wad of towels. "Please wait in here," the Governess told the girls. "I'll go and find out what happens next."

Failure sat down in a chair heavily, while Doom perched on the high lab stool like a love bird. She trembled a little, the tissues in her hands quivering as though in a breeze.

"Sorry you lost your Anchor," Failure said quietly.

Doom turned to look at her, her eyes shining with tears. "You mean sorry that *you* lost my Anchor," she retorted in a quivering voice, white hot with fury. "Anyway, she isn't lost."

"Well… she is," Failure corrected. "She made a break for it. Hence, you've lost your Anchor."

"No. She's still somewhere on the Island," Doom replied, taking a great shuddering breath. "The entire Island will become my Anchor."

Failure gaped at the girl in horror. "You aren't still going to try and travel, are you?"

"I most certainly am," Doom corrected. "I'm not missing out. Not because of this slip-up."

"But you haven't had a chance to practice with the island as your Anchor," Failure stalled.

"It's a pretty big Anchor to aim for," Doom replied. "I feel happy with it. If I didn't, I wouldn't try again."

Failure got to her feet and paced away from Doom. "Ok," she said, turning and standing tall before her. "I know you don't like me. And honestly; I don't like you. But I'm here to help you. Actually, I'm here to save your life. So, you're going to have to listen to me."

A curious expression crossed Doom's face, and then, to Failure's horror, she began to laugh her tinkling bell of a laugh.

"To save my life?!" she cried. "Well, that's very noble of you, but I'm absolutely fine as I am, thank you. And if I wanted anybody to save my life, I wouldn't be giving the job to you."

Failure needed to explain it all. She needed to show Doom the white statues, distorted in agony. She needed to explain about the Galilei and the destructive ambition of the Programme. But the light was beginning to wane, and at sundown, Doom was going to die. And so instead of trying to explain a single thing more, Failure pulled out the polished wood of the crossbow she had taken from Pa's weapon's cabinet. "I'm really sorry about this," Failure said, as the colour drained from Doom's face. "But you have to do what I say."

"You want to steal my thunder," Doom uttered, her face vivid with rage.

"What? Don't be insane," Failure hissed. "We only have a couple of minutes. We need to get you out of here."

"You want to be the only one who has touched time," Doom went on, stepping down from her stool. "You don't want me to shine and have the glory you think is yours."

"If you carry on like this, I'm seriously just gonna put the goddam bolt in your brains and be done with it," Failure snapped, moving closer to the girl. "And keep your voice down or they're going to hear—"

But before she could finish her sentence, Doom had leapt forward and kicked Failure's ankle out from under her. White bursts of sickening agony blinded Failure, as Doom grabbed the stool and swung it at Failure's body, knocking the crossbow from her hands. It dropped at her feet with a clang. Doom scrambled for the weapon as, through the starry mania of pain, Failure managed to kick the bow, which skidded across the white lab floor. Doom leapt for it, but Failure grabbed the girl's shin, sending her slamming to the floor. She leapt on top of Doom and pinned her neck to the ground.

"You have to listen to me!" Failure hissed, covering Doom's mouth. "I swear I don't give a jack-snap-shut about your glory or thunder or whatever. If you make that attempt to travel today, then you're going to die. I've seen it. In the future of today." A wrench of fear passed through Doom's eyes. Failure removed her hand from the girl's mouth. "The Travelling attempts aren't safe," Failure went on. "Kids have died. You die. I'm here to stop that happening."

"You're saying that Conductor VI doesn't work," Doom snapped, still pinned. "But you're also claiming to have travelled here through time? That doesn't work. Both can't be true."

"I didn't come here by that death trap," Failure told her. "I came with this." She fished the Galilei she had stolen from classroom twelve from her pocket and Doom's eyes widened in disbelief.

"It's really, really complicated, and there isn't time to explain," Failure went on. "But why else would I have a Galilei, and show you that I have it? I'd be expelled for this. And much worse. If you want to live, you have to trust me. If you can't trust me, then I can't save you." Failure let the girl go.

Doom sat up, her face a knot of confusion and doubt. At last, she asked, "Say it's all true. Say you're here to rescue me – what's your plan, exactly?"

"I'm going to put on a lab coat and grab some equipment," Failure said. "Then I'm going to walk out of this murder dome in plain sight and hope that no one gives me a second glance. You do the same."

"That's a terrible plan," Doom said, shaking her head. She climbed to her feet and began to pace. "Every eye is on me. I won't get out of this room without being put back on the Conductor. That's a certainty. But there could be another way of me getting out of here."

"How?" Failure asked.

"There's a grill, right behind the Conductor. I think it's an air vent. Kimsha climbed up there earlier when some idiot had let go of her lead. That was when they insisted on her being in a cage. The vent would be big enough to climb through, and it's only a few feet off the ground. If you can kick the grill off from the outside, then I can climb out of it when I should be making the attempt."

"But they'll all be watching you."

"No," Doom shook her head. "The actual attempt happens behind an enormous screen, to protect the rest of them from radiation. It's a huge blast and it lasts for about thirty seconds. I'll have to get out of the machine and climb up through the vent. When the screen pulls back up, I'll be gone. Successful traveller number seven."

"But won't they strap you in?" Failure asked, as a key began to sound in the lock of the door.

"Yes, they will," Doom replied, and the frosty, perfect smile snapped back across her face. "But I'm gifted, adaptive and fearless. So don't worry about me."

The door was opened by a Governess, who signalled to Failure, "You need to go to the infirmary."

"Yes Miss," Failure replied. She looked back at Doom, who met her gaze with surprising clarity and cool.

"See you on the other side," Doom said with a wicked smile.

Failure followed the Governess and emerged into the gathering dusk and, heart hammering, pretended to stride away back to the main building. Instead, Failure hurried around the perimeter of the dome, seeking the grill that would be Doom's escape.

At last she found it, glinting silver in the dying light. But such was the lie of the land on which the dome had been built, that whilst inside Doom could reach it with ease, here on the outside the grill was fifteen feet above the ground.

There's no chance of me reaching that, Failure told her guts. *Doom's trapped.*

A wave of cold sweat broke out on Failure's skin, but once again her guts made no reply.

From within the Dome, a low hum sounded. An announcement commenced on a raspy Tannoy, wobbling its way towards her through the air vent. A countdown. They had already begun the attempt.

I'll just have to charge in there and stop them, she thought. *I still have the grenades I nicked from Pa.*

The grenades. Failure reached inside her pockets and drew out the first. The countdown ended. A whirring, clicking sound came from inside. The ground at Failure's feet began to thrum. The Conductor was alive. Doom would be hidden from view by the protective radiation shield. She would be fighting free of the straps. Failure gripped the first grenade, pulled out the pin, squeezed down on the trigger then raised her arm. She hurled the grenade at the tiny grate on the vast wall of the Dome.

Failure was thrown violently backwards as the explosion rent through the air. The grill and the wall of the Dome around it was smashed to a thousand pieces. Failure landed on the wet turf with a smack, curling up in a ball as rubble rained down upon her.

When she dared to uncover her head, a great wall of smoke was drifting over her, slow and thick and hot. From the shimmering glass panels of the dome, black smoke was billowing up into the sky: the entire thing was on the verge of collapse. As the wall of smoke that engulfed her passed, it exposed an enormous, jagged, angry hole. Through the smoke seeping from within, a silhouette emerged. Her face, body and hands were blackened with soot, her mouth wide open in shock. Behind her, the protective screen was being hammered on manually, and the sound of chaos and panic reigned in the dome beyond.

Doom jumped down into the pile of rubble below her, whilst Failure shook herself free and, wincing, climbed to her feet. "You're alive, ok," Failure called, as Doom stamped across the debris towards her.

"So, you really do go around blowing things up," Doom said with a fierce grin.

"I don't really mean to," Failure frowned. "I've just had a strange month."

"Luckily for me," said Doom. "Got any more of those things?" Doom held a hand out, palm facing up, a bright intensity in her face. Failure nodded and placed the second grenade in her outstretched hand. "Then let's raze this thing to the ground."

Together, the girls turned back to the Dome and hurled their explosives. Then ran for their lives.

CHAPTER THIRTY-NINE

At the summit of the cliff, the girls paused to catch their breath. The stars were winking in the sky above, and the moon shone brightly. In the distance, the wreckage of the Dome billowed with plumes of black smoke, which was beginning to blot out the stars. Failure thought of home.

"So, whoever made it out of that Dome thinks I've either just been radiated into tiny pieces or travelled through time," Doom panted, leaning her hands on her knees. "Either way, I'm safe as long as they don't see me. Which is not ideal when I'm trapped on a tiny island."

"Don't worry," Failure said between ragged breaths, "I already have a plan."

"Oh great," Doom said with a curl of her cupids bow lips. "Another of your excellent plans. I'm sure this will be both safe and subtle."

Failure couldn't help but laugh, pointing out to sea, where the amber lights of the supply vessel were approaching the landing beach. "You need to hide up here until that supply boat lands. A storm will start while they're loading it. They panic and get careless."

"Meaning I can easily slip on board?" Doom asked.

"Exactly," Failure nodded. "Climb into one of the laundry bins. There's an officer called Smith on board who will come for you. He's a good guy. He's expecting to find me hiding in there. But I know him, and I know he'll get you somewhere safe."

"He's expecting you?" Doom asked, peering at Failure curiously in the moonlight, eyes bright above her soot smeared cheeks and nose. "So, it's you who's meant to be escaping?"

"Yeah," Failure said with a sigh, "but who gives a goddam?" Failure's words were spliced by the blaring scream of a distant alarm.

"It's ok, that's just me... the other me," Failure explained, "I've just nicked the Galilei and set off the alarms. In fact, we need to get ourselves hidden," she added urgently. "The other me is gonna be coming this way in a while with the others and none of them can see us. But we need to stay in sight of the beach."

"Get in behind here," Doom said, grabbing Failure's hand and leading her to a dense growth of thorny briar. They crawled painstakingly in behind the shadowed thorns and hunkered down.

"I won't forget this, Failure," Doom said, her voice brittle with determination. "And one day I'll repay you. I swear it."

Together, the girls shivered as the alarm died on the wind and the supply boat drew nearer. A fine mist of drizzle began to fall in the cold night. Through the dense thicket, a small group of shadows were just visible approaching the cliff edge.

"I think that's me from earlier," Failure whispered. "Yes, look, there's your tiger cub."

"Kimsha?" Doom gasped in a strangled whisper.

"We can't be seen by anyone. Or interfere. It's dangerous." But even as her words died on the gathering rain, Failure had a strange, unsteady feeling. She remembered a ghostly voice, calling the name Kimsha on the wind and in the rain. So, there were ghosts on the island of Eylan Morr, after all. But they were the ghosts of the future, not of the dead.

"Call her," Failure told Doom.

"What?" Doom cried. "You just told me—"

"Please, trust me, just call her, she'll come!"

Doom took a deep breath and gently called, "Kiiiiiiiimmm-shaaaaahhhh," onto the breeze. And again, "Kiiiiiiiimmm-shaaaaahhhh."

Moments later, with a scramble and a slash of claw, the snuffling nose and wide black eyes of the tiger cub scrambled towards them through the thicket. Doom held out loving arms and the tiger thrust itself into her embrace.

"Thank you, Failure," Doom said earnestly, the tiger cub nuzzled in her arms like an infant, tear tracks of joy etched on her cheeks. "I owe you my whole life."

"Yeah, well, I'm a big hero," Failure muttered. "I hope you make it."

Failure watched the girl and the cub as they made their way down the cliff path in the rain. As she reached the beach, Doom strode confidently through the chaotic scene, invisible in the panic. She dropped the tiger cub into the first empty wooden crate she came to and secured it with a lid. She lifted the crate and walked up the gangplank without an apparent care in the world, disappearing into the boat, and to freedom. Failure's escape plan had worked. Just not for her.

CHAPTER FORTY

The rainstorm had puttered out to a drizzling mist by the time Failure reached the lighthouse. Tor was waiting for her, pacing back and forth.

"She's ok," Failure said quickly as she stepped over the threshold, "I did it. She's alive."

Tor flung her arms around Failure and the girls embraced tightly. "You did it, Failure," Tor breathed, as they stood apart. "You really did it. Did she make it onto the boat?"

"Yep, all safe and sound," Failure replied. "She's in Smith's hands now. And there's something else. We kind of blew up the Conductor."

Tor stared back at Failure with wide eyes. "That'll explain the bang, then," she replied, and the girls laughed. "Let's go and take a look."

"What did Desi do when he got back?" Failure asked, as the girls headed out of the lighthouse. Tor stopped. She looked up at Failure.

"Isn't he with you?" she asked.

"No, he said to get back to the lighthouse," Failure explained. "The Galilei was having a hard time bringing us back, I think the time was running out. So, he pulled his hands out of mine and we came separately."

The sudden pale dread on Tor's face told Failure all that she needed to know.

"He couldn't have made it back without you," Tor told her, quietly. "If he let go of your hands then the link was broken."

"Then where is he?" Failure asked, her words choking her. "Stuck back there, a month ago?"

"Not if you had already started the travelling," Tor shook her head. "He must have been flung out. Some when in time. But I couldn't ever tell you where or when. He's gone."

Failure stared at Tor as the warm wind whipped the windows of the lighthouse, as the cold night grew ever darker, as the distant smoke obliterated the moon. Failure looked out over the Atlantic Ocean which shushed like a comforting mother all around. Black waves slammed onto the fortress of rocks that was Eylan Morr. In the sky above the distant plateau, a vulture circled on the warm currents of the wind.

"He sent me back to save her," Failure said through silent tears, which drove clean streaks down her soot smothered cheeks. "And that's what I've done. But there's one more life that needs saving tonight. Come on."

The cages in the yard were hushed with snuffling and slumber. Failure left Tor standing in the doorway as look out. First, she found the central grill through which she herself had escape the walls of the Programme at night. She dragged the grill away, revealing the tunnel beneath it which led to the beyond. Leaving the gaping black hole in the floor, she approached the bars of the cage on the far side of the quad.

Hot, rancid breath steamed from within and a shuffling of claw and fur sounded. Failure pressed a hand to the bars. She turned her face up towards the sky and parted her lips, tasting the last mist of rain, laced with gunpowder and molten gold. Licking and pursing her lips, Failure turned to the cage and whispered, "Failure." With a hot flash of amber, a pair of eyes sought her from the darkness. They radiated their toxic light, blinked and came closer.

"I've got a crossbow on me," Failure said in a hushed voice, "and my friend's over there at the door. So, if you try any funny business, I'll shoot you in the face and she'll lock you back here in this cage. They'll carry on all those things they've been doing to you. So be smart." Failure stepped back from the cage and loaded her crossbow. "Get yourself back in the sea and find a new town. Or go home. Just don't come back here. Swift wind, m'love."

Failure unlocked the bolts which secured the cage. She backed away, crossbow raised. From the shadows, the Sylkie emerged. Her black and golden fur prickled and gleamed in the moonlight. Yellow saliva dripped from her jaws, and a growl emanated from her throat. She walked like a dog that has been battered down until its spirit is broken. Tentative. Slow. Lopsided gait and tense limbs. The legacy of her treatment. But still the light shone in her eyes. She looked up at Failure one last time and growled low, before slinking across to the tunnel in the concrete floor and vanishing.

On the plateau, students were milling about in a state of disorder, still dressed in their evening gowns and suits, high heeled shoes in hands, huddling together and questioning and gawping. The enormous pile of rubble which had been the Conductor was billowing with smoke and crackling with dying fire.

"Quite a show, Failure, ain't it?" Ness and his knot were passing by, making their way down towards the wreckage of the Conductor, all wide eyed, thrilled and horrified at the same time.

"Yeah, it's a goddam party," Failure replied.

"They're saying that Doom might have made it, though," Ness told her. "And that Despair LeoMontague is responsible for all this mess. But of course, you would already know that, seeing as he was the one who gave you all those nasty bruises."

"Dunno what you mean," Failure said, touching the skin of her face, where she had earlier smashed the clock against it.

"He went missing, apparently," Ness explained. "Same time as someone broke into the LatLong classroom and stole a very valuable Galilei. Attacked you in order to make his escape, according to the Governess. Well, everyone knows you two weren't exactly getting along. Seems like he then made the rather rash decision to blow up the Conductor, trying to prevent Doom from Travelling away, perhaps. Or just covering his tracks as he made his escape. Either way, he's gone. They're out there looking for him now," Ness added.

"Good luck to them," Tor said, "I hope they find him. Long live the Kala."

"Why would he want the Galilei for himself, though?" Failure asked, feeling a deep pang of guilt that Desi's memory would forever be reduced, unfairly, to thief and terrorist.

"Only time will tell," Ness shrugged. "Nothing to do with you, of course," he added quietly, inclining his head.

"Nothing at all," Failure replied. "How could it?"

"That's the question," Ness smiled. "But tonight, I think we'll just enjoy the fireworks, eh?"

For a moment, Failure watched as Ness and his knot wandered toward the smoking heap of rubble. Far above, the smoke was already dissipating, the dim silver twinkle of the stars emerging in the pre-dawn sky. With a flutter of wings, something sharp and painful dug into Failure's shoulder. With a wince and a yell, Failure ducked and then found her feet, recognising the beady black eyes and white and yellow plumage of the bird who had landed so deftly upon her, claiming her as her own.

"Kezia," she breathed, her heart tearing inside her. The bird only stared about at the wreckage.

Failure and Tor began to wander slowly back toward the main buildings through the carnage, the white bird perched upon Failure's shoulder.

"What do we do now?" Failure asked.

"Come up with another escape plan, I suppose," Tor frowned. "Although I have a funny feeling things are going to change around here after tonight. What would your mother have done, d'you suppose?"

"You'd know better than me," Failure replied, and was surprised to feel unbidden salt grit tears in her eyes once again. "I'd kind of like to... would it be ok if you sort of tell me stuff about her. Not tonight, I mean. Just sometime."

"Of course," Tor replied. "And in terms of what's to come next – Just remember what she said in that letter. 'Whatever comes of your gifts, be they many, few or none, use them with your heart, and use them kindly.' I guess that's the best road map you have for what's to come."

"What d'you mean, 'what's to come'?" Failure asked.

"Revolution," Tor replied, her pale blue eyes sparkling. "Oh, and the end of the world, of course."

Failure began to laugh. The first morning sunlight burst over the lip of the horizon and flooded the world in its golden glow. Failure tilted her head back in its warmth.

It's like Eylan Morr's trying to remind me that I'm not home, after all. Failure told her guts. Yet again, they made no reply.

Why have you gone so goddam quiet? Failure demanded furiously of her guts, her heart, her pocket watch, the sky, the sea and the stars. She stood still for a moment as a hot, dry wind rose in the air and the rush of the waves sounded below.

"I can't hear you anymore!" Failure cried aloud, frantically into the wind. "Don't leave me on my own." Her voice was lifted by a hot current and whipped around the girl and the vulture upon her shoulder, flowing across the grassland, past the Perimeter and through the standing stones, out over the open ocean, where it splintered and scattered away. Ahead, Tor paused amidst the flow of the crowd and glanced back, hearing the cry. Failure smiled as she walked toward her friend.

ABOUT THE AUTHOR

Kitty is a writer, composer and lyricist with years of experience working in theatre and television with a number of published works under her belt.

Kitty grew up in a rural Suffolk village near Bury St Edmunds, where she and her brothers spent their time making up stories, making comics, fantasy worlds and inventing games. At Birmingham University, she studied a BA Hons in Drama and Theatre Arts and a masters degree in Playwriting, before moving to South East London to persue her writing career.

She now lives in Essex with her husband and two young sons. Kitty loves good pubs, elegant cocktail bars, country rambling, late night karaoke, and going on adventures with her family.

DAVID BARKER

PAX

AND THE MISSING HEAD

Illustrated by Bruna Oliveira Marini

You may also enjoy...

WHEN A TRAGIC PAST POSSESSES THE PRESENT, ONLY ONE GIRL CAN SET THEM FREE.
THE EXCITING AND SPOOKY DEBUT FROM WRITER SARA LAMERTON.

THE CURSE OF DRAKE'S ISLAND

SARA LAMERTON

An exciting read from Donn Swaby...

www.ingramcontent.com/pod-product-compliance
Lightning Source LLC
Chambersburg PA
CBHW031955240626
47153CB00003B/1001